'I keep misjudging you.'

His harshly muttered admission broke into her thoughts. 'I beg your pardon?'

Gabe paused and reached out a hand to take her arm and turn her to face him. Leith felt again the sudden flare of awareness that his touch had evoked on the plane, and wondered if he felt the tremors that flickered and fluttered through her body.

'I don't usually make snap judgements about people, but I seem to have done that with you. You keep throwing me completely off balance. . .'

Dear Reader

This month we complete Margaret O'Neill's quartet with TAKE A DEEP BREATH, based around the accident and emergency department. We go to Australia with Lilian Darcy in NO MORE SECRETS, where the need to conceal Thea's romance with Joe leads to problems, and introduce a new Australian author in Meredith Webber, whose HEALING LOVE takes us to a burns unit in India—Leith and Gabe are fascinating people. We round up with TILL SUMMER ENDS by Hazel Fisher—warm thoughts as we move into spring!

The Editor

Having pursued many careers—from school-teaching to pig farming—with varying degrees of success and plenty of enjoyment, **Meredith Webber** seized on the arrival of a computer in her house as an excuse to turn to what had always been a secret urge—writing. Having more doctors and nurses in the family than any other professional people, the medical romance seemed the way to go! Meredith lives on the Gold Coast of Queensland, with her husband and teenage son.

HEALING LOVE

BY
MEREDITH WEBBER

MILLS & BOON

MILLS & BOON LIMITED
ETON HOUSE, 18–24 PARADISE ROAD
RICHMOND, SURREY, TW9 1SR

All the characters in this book have no existence outside the imagination of the Author, and have no relation whatsoever to anyone bearing the same name or names. They are not even distantly inspired by any individual known or unknown to the Author, and all the incidents are pure invention.

All Rights Reserved. The text of this publication or any part thereof may not be reproduced or transmitted in any form or by any means, electronic or mechanical, including photocopying, recording, storage in an information retrieval system, or otherwise, without the written permission of the publisher.

This book is sold subject to the condition that it shall not, by way of trade or otherwise, be lent, resold, hired out or otherwise circulated without the prior consent of the publisher in any form of binding or cover other than that in which it is published and without a similar condition including this condition being imposed on the subsequent purchaser.

*First published in Great Britain 1994
by Mills & Boon Limited*

© Meredith Webber 1994

*Australian copyright 1994
Philippine copyright 1994
This edition 1994*

ISBN 0 263 78479 7

*Set in 10 on 12 pt Linotron Times
03-9403-52285*

*Typeset in Great Britain by Centracet, Cambridge
Made and printed in Great Britain*

CHAPTER ONE

'BLUNDERING destiny!'

'Yours or mine?' Even as she asked the rhetorical question, Leith Robinson kept her eyes on the deft, gloved fingers of the surgeon, ready to anticipate his every need. The swift pang his words had caused was hidden from his intent eyes. Had it been destiny that turned her life around, or her own 'blundering'?

'It's not personal; that's why it blunders.' Ian's voice was strangely disembodied, muffled by the surgical mask.

'I always thought "blind" was a better description.' Tim Waters was the anaesthetist who, with the scout, made up their team in the theatre of the busy day hospital. The conversations over the inert and semi-comatose bodies of their patients ranged from deep philosophical debate to puerile nonsense.

'Now there's a word we don't use in this theatre. Wrap this one up, will you, please, Leith? Tim and I shall continue this discussion over a hot cuppa while you wheel in the next one.'

Ian Musgrave wandered from the room, peeling off the disposable trappings of his trade and hurling them towards the refuse bin as he left. He was a large, shambling figure of a man, clumsy in every aspect of his life apart from his work, where his fingers performed a special magic of their own, restoring the fading sight of thousands of people a year.

With firm but gentle pressure Leith fixed a patch

over the patient's eye, then pressed the bell for a nurse from the recovery-room to take over.

A long day stretched ahead—the operating list included six cataract removals and four minor procedures.

'We settled on "blindly blundering",' Ian informed her genially as he accompanied the next cataract patient through the door, his local anaesthetic already administered in the ante-room.

'Leith won't agree, will you, my dear?' Ian held up his hands for the gloves she had ready, then turned for her to tie on his mask. 'There's no such thing as destiny in your ordered life, is there?'

His eyelid dropped swiftly in a wink, including her in the bantering fun that lightened the strain of their work.

'Unless you count Gabe Vincent as destiny?' Tim queried.

'I thought he was the Archangel, not God,' she responded, 'and where, if a humble nurse might ask, does he fit into this conversation?'

'We've just had tea with him. He's using the other theatre this week. Actually, he asked if he could borrow you for tomorrow.' Ian made a small slit in the tough tissue of the cornea as he answered, and delicately extracted the damaged, opaque lens, leaving the tiny capsule intact.

'And what did you say to that?' She asked the question quietly, her mind on her work, her fingers passing the needle holder to him at the same time.

'I told him that you were not mine to lend, more's the pity, but if he wanted to speak to you personally you would be through here at about seven o'clock.'

'And probably on the look-out for someone to buy you dinner,' Tim chimed in.

'Stop your nonsense, both of you. Is any of this true?'

'Would we lie to you? We, who love you like——'

'A sister?'

'I was going to say mother!'

She chuckled helplessly at their irrepressible slapstick humour. 'Men!' she muttered. 'I'll throw a tray of instruments at you one of these days. Setting me up like this!'

'It's not a set-up. The Archangel Gabriel himself has come down off his cloud to request your services,' said Tim cheekily.

'He's a brilliant surgeon, Tim, and he's had enough personal tragedy to excuse a certain aloofness.' Ian's voice held a note of reproof.

'I don't mind his aloofness; it's his speciality that bugs me. Fancy making your money out of women's vanity.'

Patients came and went, but the small talk rarely skipped a beat.

'There's more to plastic surgery than face-lifts, you know,' Ian reproved them both. He was invariably fair-minded. Although she agreed with Tim, Leith decided it was time to drag their conversation back to the original topic.

'Will you two please stop your private bickering and answer my question? Why did Dr Vincent ask for me? The second theatre has its own list of emergency help that it can call up if someone's going to be away.'

'He's heard about the special magic in your fingers when you sli-i-i-ide our gloves on.' Their differences forgotten, they were off again, indulging their passion for patter!

'And the intoxication of your wa-a-arm sweet breath when you reach up to tie on our masks.'

'Hold it right there!' she ordered, her mask concealing a grin. 'Why I put up with you two, with your sexist remarks and schoolboy humour, I don't know! Working for Dr Vincent might be a pleasant change.'

'We're not on duty tomorrow anyway. You'd be doing corns and bunions for Gracie.'

'If you had bad feet, you might show Dr Grace more respect.'

'If I had bad feet, I wouldn't show them to Gracie!'

Leith smiled, secure in her position as part of this team. It was a rare camaraderie they shared, three people, cut off by the sterile whiteness of the theatre, lightening the load of their work with facetious humour, while they performed their tasks with professional expertise.

The bright glare of the lights overhead held dusk at bay, and only an increasing weariness signalled that the day was nearly over.

Checking the schedule, Leith saw that this was the last patient for the day. Mr Groves was an elderly man in for an ectropion operation — one of the simple tasks usually listed at the end. Tim administered the mild anaesthetic, then left the room to check on the previous case.

'A day in theatre with Gabe Vincent would do you no harm.' Ian broke the silence that always lengthened with the day. 'It's added experience, and he's certainly one of the best in his field.'

'He hasn't asked me yet!' Tiredness lent an edge to

her voice, making it sound more abrupt than she had intended.

'He won't threaten your careful façade of indifference, Leith. He's too wrapped up in his own private cocoon of misery.'

She glanced up swiftly at this perceptive man, who rarely strayed from the role of colleague, yet knew and understood so much about her.

'I knew his wife,' she told him quietly, steering the conversation away from herself. 'Katherine and I went to the same school. She was older than me, but so beautiful and kind—every one loved her. I——'

She was diverted by a bright head that popped round the door.

'Doctor Vincent would like a word with you when you finish, Leith. He's waiting in the tea-room, but said to tell you there's no hurry.'

'Thanks, Anne. I'll be at least half an hour by the time I've scrubbed down here.' She turned back to her work, the judgemental remark that she had been about to utter cut off by the interruption.

'You, of all people, should not judge others on hearsay.' Ian had read her thoughts correctly and rebuked her mildly, so that she flushed with shame, her soft brown eyes lifting to his in consternation.

'I *was* going to judge, I suppose, but I cannot understand the moral and ethical values of a man who would countenance cosmetic surgery for his wife when she was dying of cancer. Surely she was in enough pain without that.'

'There's been too much gossip about that situation. Now that Katherine is dead, no one but Gabe himself could know the reasons for their decision, and he sure as hell won't discuss it.'

'You're too good to be true if you didn't even wonder about it!' she said tartly, discomfited by his censure.

'I'm not saying I didn't wonder. I'm simply saying that too many people jump to wrong conclusions in our incestuous little world of medicine.' He waggled a gloved finger at her. 'I'm asking you to keep an open mind, and listen to Gabe without preconceived ideas cluttering up your thought processes.'

'I hear you, o master!' She bowed across the table at him, a hidden smile lighting up her tired eyes.

'Don't get cheeky!' he responded gruffly. 'That's the last, isn't it?'

'Yes. I'll finish up if you want to get going.'

'I'm not in a hurry, and there's something I want to say to you.' Ian finished his work and waited while the scout wheeled the patient out. As she peeled off her gloves, then reached up to untie her mask, she watched him with wary eyes.

'Well?'

She was aware of her own defensiveness. It created a barrier between them, but, even with Ian, she could not easily lower her guard.

'It's twelve months since you had that accident, Leith, and ten months since you came to work here, so quiet and pale, it was like having a shadowy ghost about the place.' He paused, as if trying to gauge her reaction, but she refused to betray any emotion as she listened to his words.

With a sigh he continued, 'What happened to you—losing the baby, then Mark going off with Caroline—were both personal tragedies, but they are in the past. Everyone needs a period of recovery, but then they must face the future—look forward, not backwards.

'You're young, and beautiful, my dear.' He paused

for a moment, letting his words sink in. 'I think it's time for you to say "that's enough convalescence" and get on with your life.'

'Do you think I don't tell myself that? Do you think I haven't tried?' she asked bitterly, rolling the discarded gloves into a ball and hurling them towards the bin. 'Who do we meet in our work, Ian? Other nurses and doctors, of course! Do you think they don't know?'

There was a clatter outside the door, but Ian stood mute, neither agreeing with nor disputing her words, until she was forced to continue.

'When I meet people, I can almost hear the conversation. "Leith Robinson?" they say. "Engaged to Mark Armstrong, wasn't she? Had a car accident and miscarried—first thing anyone knew about her being pregnant!"'

'It was a nine-day wonder, Leith. I know it must have hurt you, but you can't let it colour your whole life.'

'Can't I, Ian? I was so happy about that baby, and so stupid. Unbelievably stupid! I thought Mark was just as delighted as I was.'

She shook her head slowly, then admitted, 'It was a mistake, of course! We'd been engaged for a year and were due to get married two months after it was confirmed. We hadn't planned to have children immediately, but I didn't think it would matter!'

Her voice pleaded for understanding.

Ian said nothing, but his murmur of agreement prompted her to continue.

'Do you know what tortures me now?' she cried, the words coming thickly from her constricted throat. 'Now I wonder if I subconsciously managed the pregnancy because I was unsure of his love.'

She pulled off her cap as she spoke, and twisted it between her fingers, glad to have something to focus on while she revealed the suspicions she had buried so deeply.

'Maybe I was trying to bind him closer to me because I sensed that he might stray,' she murmured, glad to have the thoughts that haunted her out in the open.

'If you keep on analysing yourself and passing such damning judgements you'll never get over those losses.' Ian's firm voice denied her doubts.

Silence strained between them, so taut that it was almost physical.

'I'll never get over them anyway, Ian.'

She spoke so quietly that he had to bend his head to hear her words—words that held a haunting, aching sadness. The fingers of her left hand moved of their own accord to touch a triangular scar at the corner of her eye, the only visible reminder of the accident.

Lost in the past, she paused for a long moment before continuing, her breath coming out with a muted sob.

'You see, Ian, what the gossip-mongers missed was the best bit of the lot—the final punishment for the crime of love.' Her voice sounded strangled in her own ears, catching in her throat as she forced the confession past cold, numb lips.

'What can be so devastating, my dear, that you could turn your back on life?' Ian's hands reached out to grasp her shoulders, and he drew her close, to rest against his broad chest.

With her face muffled against him, she unburdened herself of the secret that had shattered her life.

'The accident caused damage to my uterus as well as killing the embryo. They told me. . .'

The horror of the crash seemed to tear through her again, blocking the words she must say. Lost in the past, she battled to control the tears that stung at her eyelids.

'Told you what, Leith? Tell me what it is that's hurting you so much.'

'They told me that I will never be able to bear another child,' she whispered, feeling again the twisting, wrenching agony of that fateful day.

'That's why Mark left, or so he said!' The words were tumbling out now, pleading for his understanding, his sympathy, even hoping for his denial of what she knew was true!

'That's what hurt so much, Ian, and why any future relationship must be in jeopardy.'

'No, Leith! You're wrong. A man would love you for yourself.'

'Do you think so, Ian?' she asked with a bitter sadness in her voice. 'Men might say they marry for love, but procreation is what marriage is all about. Men reach a stage in their lives when they want a wife and children—it's a package deal that's taken for granted!'

She took a deep breath, then went on, 'If Mark, who really loved me, felt that way, what other man would be likely to want a woman who can't bear his children?'

Tears that had been held back for too long dampened his rough jacket as Ian held her close. Despite the utter despair in her voice, she felt the relief that confession brought, and was warmed and comforted by Ian's soothing murmurs and clumsy pats.

'Not having a child is not the end of the world, Leith,' he said huskily, obviously affected by her story.

She raised her head, regarding him steadily as she wiped away the damp reminders of her misery.

'It shouldn't be, I know,' she replied, her voice still full of tears. 'I also know that my life would be meaningless without children. It's just the way I am. We could have adopted, but Mark hated that idea, and so—well. . .'

Ian held her close, until the shuddering sobs that racked her body had died to an occasional hiccup.

'Don't judge all men by Mark,' he told her quietly, but the words lacked conviction, and she knew he was considering what his own reaction would have been.

She paused while she collected her thoughts, then her sense of humour came again to her rescue, relieving the tension between them, and signalling to Ian that she was feeling easier in her mind.

'Well, it's all over now. As it happened, Caroline had been in the shadows for a long time and no doubt has a perfect womb, just right for bearing hundreds of little Armstrongs.'

Ian hugged her once more, a firm, hard gesture of sympathy, admiration and support.

'I'm glad you told me, Leith. It just proves my point that we shouldn't judge other people too hastily.' He grinned at her. 'Now, wash your face and go listen to what Gabe Vincent has to say.'

'I will, and thanks. I'm sorry to have held you up.'

She pushed him towards the door, her affection for this sensible man warming her aching muscles and weary bones. He might fool around with Tim, and tease her unmercifully, but he had her interests at heart, and she would trust his judgement in anything.

Thirty minutes had stretched to sixty by the time she finished her duties. Slipping out of the thin cotton shift she wore under her theatre gown, she pulled on the jeans and checked shirt that she had worn to work.

Trust you to be wearing your scruffiest clothes at a time like this, she told herself, picking ineffectually at the small spots of paint that decorated the denim.

Hurriedly rinsing the tear stains off her cheeks, she grimaced at her pale reflection. The hours she worked meant that she rarely saw the sun, and the long day in Theatre had left her looking unhealthily washed out.

Her soft golden-brown hair was flat and lifeless after its day tucked under a cap. There was no time to worry about make-up, but she wasn't going anywhere with hair like that! Gabe Vincent would have to wait another few minutes!

She bent forward and brushed it vigorously away from her head, enjoying the sharpness of the bristles against her scalp and feeling the blood rushing into her face.

'I don't want to hurry you, but I think they want to lock up.'

She looked up at the sound of the deep voice, pushing tousled hair out of her eyes, suddenly conscious of her flushed cheeks and dishevelled appearance.

Her honey-brown eyes met others of a startling blue. Shock-waves spiralled through her, leaving her with a feeling of intense vulnerability that was almost fear.

'Dr Vincent.' She swallowed the 'I presume' that leapt automatically to her lips. 'I'm sorry I've kept you waiting.'

With a nervous hand she patted her hair into place, thrusting her brush deep into her shoulder-bag as she spoke. What did he want with her?

Curiosity about his motives made her examine more

closely the man who had, until now, been simply another of the many specialists she had passed in the corridors of the hospital.

He was taller than she remembered — she was above average height herself, but had to tilt her head back to study a face that gave nothing away. Taller, and more athletic, somehow, she thought, as he turned and walked with a lithe stride towards the front door. The broadness of his shoulders might owe something to the tailoring of his jacket, but, noting the muscular calves that his well-cut trousers did little to conceal, she rather doubted it.

Lost in her inventory, she followed him automatically.

'The name's Gabe.'

He threw the words over his shoulder, then paused to hold the door open for her. 'You've had a long day. If we go across to Michael's, we could have a drink or a cup of coffee while we talk.'

She glanced up at him suspiciously. Had Tim dared to suggest that she would want a dinner invitation?

His dark face seemed set in a mask of indifference, an unyielding geometry of muscle and bone, with the olive skin of his Italian ancestry stretched tautly across the framework. Thick black hair shone dully under the street-light as his hand reached out for her elbow and he guided her across the street.

She felt her body's slight response to his touch, a signal of awareness between male and female. Perhaps Ian was right! Perhaps it was time to put the past behind her, she thought wryly.

Her physical reaction and the thoughts it evoked frightened her, and she hesitated on the footpath, instinctively glancing into the darkened glass of the café windows to see if she looked as scruffy as she felt.

Her short hair hung in a tousled cap about her face. In the dark glass it looked quite fashionable, but she was certain that in the brighter light of the café it would just appear untidy!

The reflection lacked colour, but she knew there were dark circles beneath her eyes, making them seem larger and more deep-set than they were. The same strain had hollowed out her cheeks, so that her bones were prominent, even in this dim mirror. She sighed softly.

Twelve months ago her even, classical features had been her one vanity, and she had known that they were enhanced, rather than diminished, by the severity of her uniform. But now. . .

'Come along, girl, I'm starving!'

His voice broke into her thoughts, prompting her to reply testily, 'You don't have to feed me. If you want me to work for you tomorrow, I'd be quite happy to do it, providing the sister on duty in that theatre is prepared to take my place.'

She paused, but when he made no response she felt compelled to continue, 'The experience would be interesting for me, but I don't see what you're hoping to achieve from it.'

'Are you always this prickly and defensive?'

'No, I——' She felt limp, wrung out, the spark of defiance quickly extinguished when he interrupted her muttered reply.

'Look, I'll explain it all to you shortly. Right now I'm tired and hungry, and so, if your tone is anything to judge by, are you. Let's go inside, sit down, and have a quick bite to eat, then we can talk. Is there anyone you should let know that you're running late?'

There was a total lack of interest in the question, a formal query of politeness, nothing more.

'No.'

The single word came out more ungraciously than she had intended. The wretched man was right—she was tired and hungry, and the thought of preparing a meal for herself in her empty, echoing house had little appeal.

They ordered immediately—bowls of fresh pasta and salad—and ate in silence, the formality of polite conversation unnecessary after the long day.

'I would like you to work with me tomorrow so that we can see if we might suit each other.'

His words startled her out of a pleasant sense of well-being engendered by the delicious food, soft lights and undemanding company.

'Why should we be interested in suiting each other?' she asked dispiritedly. 'I'm happy with the theatre lists I do. I can't take on any more work.'

She was aware of the constant nagging tiredness she had been feeling lately, probably as a result of the part-time job at the casino that filled her spare time at weekends.

'I don't need a theatre sister here.' He waved a hand impatiently. 'I need someone really first-class to come to India with me. It was suggested that you might be interested.'

'India? Me? With you?'

It wasn't the most intelligent conversation she'd had lately, but it was all she could muster. She looked across the table at him in amazement, seeking an answer in the shadowed angles of his face.

'Do you remember reading about an explosion in a chemical plant outside Madras about twelve months ago?' He plucked the single carnation from its vase on the table as he spoke and was absently twirling it between his fingers.

'It rings a vague bell. The place turned into an inferno in seconds, and hundreds of people were trapped.' She paled at the thought of the agony of those unknown victims.

'One hundred and seventy people were killed and another sixty-odd escaped, but many of them died and others suffered horrific burns.' The head of the flower nodded towards her as he used it to emphasise his point.

'I don't suppose any hospital in the world is prepared for disasters of that magnitude.'

'Ours are getting there. We're stockpiling material for burns suites in certain locations, and working with emergency services on a national plan. We also have our expertise for skin transplants in most bigger hospitals.'

'What happened to the people burnt in the explosion?'

She had been watching his fingers as they toyed with the flower. Long and tapering, they moved restlessly, and something in their unchecked energy sent a slight shiver down her spine. Their movement was so at odds with the careful control she heard in his voice and saw in his face.

'Many of the survivors were badly scarred. Their local doctors have done a great deal of remedial surgery, especially on their hands and feet.'

His eyes dropped to the flower, and, as if suddenly conscious of the damage his fingers might do to it, he pushed it back into the vase. His eyes remained lowered and his hands kneaded each other as he finished his explanation.

'In a land of such poverty, hands and feet are important — even if it is only so one can get about and beg.'

She was touched by the bitter compassion in his voice.

'You're going over to help?' She looked across the table at him. Her eyes, warmed by the thought of his generosity, shone in the candlelight that was drawing glints and gleams of gold from her hair.

'I'm not doing it out of kindness.' He had heard the admiration in her tone and quickly disabused her. 'The American parent company, Carew Chemicals, has paid a large amount of compensation. Some of this has gone directly to the victims or their families. Another amount has been set aside for further medical expenses.'

'Even if you are being paid, it's hardly a wise career move to go off to India to do cosmetic surgery on burn patients,' she murmured drily.

She thought a smile might be tugging at his lips, but on those sharply defined features it was hard to tell. Certainly, when he spoke of his work, his deep voice lost the curt edge that she had taken for indifference.

'Let's just say I have my reasons, not the least of which is that the money being offered is quite phenomenal, which brings me to your place in all this.'

Her breath caught in an audible gasp as she realised the implications of his words.

'Is there a sign on the hospital bulletin board saying "Leith Robinson will do anything for money"?' she enquired huffily.

'Won't you?' he countered.

'No, I won't, Dr Vincent!' she said fiercely. 'I'm damn good at my job and I don't mind how hard I work. I'm also a professional, and I'm entitled to be well paid for my services.'

The heat of a righteous anger spread through her, and she felt it burning in her cheeks.

'I agree with you completely,' he responded crisply. 'That's why I thought this job might interest you. Worked out in Australian dollars, you would be getting nine hundred a week after tax and an additional two hundred a week living-away-from-home allowance.'

'But that's immoral! Why pay a foreign nurse that amount of money when it should be going to the people themselves?'

'Because, to quote your own words, you are damn good at your job. You will earn every penny. It isn't worked out on a weekly basis, but on a lump sum,' he explained. 'When the compensation figure was decided, it would have been calculated on specialist wages for about six months. Do you understand what would have to be done?'

The abrupt change in conversation caught her off guard, and she thought for a moment.

'Not really!' she admitted. 'I suppose it would depend on the severity of the burns and how they were treated at the time. Whatever happened, I'm certain that scar tissue would have formed.'

'You're right there, and in people with darker skin the commonest form is keloid scarring. This occurred even with those victims who received transplants early, because the wounds attract extra blood supply and with it an extra supply of collagen.'

She felt his eyes on her, weighing and assessing.

Checking to see if I can understand his big words, she thought mischievously, her anger fading as she was caught up in professional interest.

'Using full-thickness skin grafts, and our improved technology, I should be able to reduce the number of operations these people will need to remove the worst of the scars.'

'And so reduce the time you would have to be over there?'

'Exactly!'

This time he did smile, and Leith was delighted by the warmth it brought to his stern mask of a face. She was musing on the effect of the smile — on her as well — when he made his point.

'I figure that, with a good nurse, I can do the job in two to three months.'

Dragging her mind away from smiles, she concentrated once more on the conversation.

'And what makes you think I'd be good enough?' The proposition excited yet dismayed her, and she wondered if he could sense the belligerence with which she masked her confusion.

'You're the best theatre nurse in the state. No one would dispute that. Believe me, I've checked around! Surgeons at Gold Coast Hospital tell me that they needed two people to fill your place when you left to join the day hospital team. I want the best, and I'm willing to pay for it.'

Bemused by his offer, and embarrassed by his words, she scrabbled in her handbag for a pen and scrap of paper. Carefully she wrote down her bring-home pay from the two jobs she was doing at the moment, adding them up and multiplying them by eight.

'Do you always do your sums before making a decision?'

She looked up at him, the faint vertical creases between her winged eyebrows indicating that her mind was still on her arithmetic.

'I can't understand figures unless they're written down.'

She looked back at her piece of paper, writing down $7,200, then adding a plus and a question mark as she calculated the possible cost of living in India.

'I could make an extra three thousand two hundred dollars in two months.' She looked back up at him, awe in her face. Another three thousand two hundred dollars closer to her goal. It would bring her dream six months closer. Her mind switched to the thought of the child that she wanted so badly, and her eyes softened.

'Do I take it that you're interested?' The deep voice mocked her, and the quick colour rose again in her cheeks, but she stifled the urge to deny his assumption, answering him with quiet dignity.

'Yes, I am, but only if you can convince me that this is the best way for the money to be spent. Whatever you or anyone else might think of me, I wouldn't like to feel I was making a profit out of other people's misery.'

She could feel her heart thudding inside her chest as she spoke, and tried to stifle the fear that threatened to engulf her. Ian was right. She had to move beyond the protective barrier she had built up around herself. Knowing that it was right, that it was time to live again, did not make it easier.

'That's a high moral consideration for someone who admits she works for money!' he said waspishly.

She flinched at the mockery in the words, but remained silent, allowing him to continue.

'The way the compensation is paid, this money would not go to the people anyway. It is specifically allocated to provide cosmetic surgery for office staff whose faces were severely burnt as a fireball swept through their section of the factory.' He paused for a moment, then obviously dismissed any concern about false modesty.

'I know I am the best person for the job, but there's no time to find and train an Indian nurse to assist me. I need a Super Sister, if you like. Without someone like that to support me, I should probably take the time that was framed in the budget, and I can't afford to be away that long.'

'I can understand that.'

She was embarrassed now that he had explained, but convinced that what he was saying was true. If he took her she would see that she earned every penny of the money that would mean so much to her.

Hiding these thoughts, she looked across at him, wishing she could see again the startling blue colour of his eyes, but the flickering shadows held their secrets.

'I'll have to speak to Dr Maxwell, who arranged my appointment with the day hospital, but I know that he would release me to go with you.' She paused for a moment before adding, 'That's if you think I'll suit.'

'We'll find that out tomorrow.'

For the next few days she swapped her duty whenever possible to work with Gabe Vincent. She might be doubtful about the type of work he did, but was forced to admire his expertise. With her interest and enthusiasm in her work rekindled, she searched through her old lecture notes for information on burns, and was studying them when the phone interrupted her.

'I thought I'd ring and see how you are. What's happening in your life, my lovely Leith?'

Had speaking to Ian of Mark last week conjured him up, like a genie from a bottle?

After a silence of twelve months his still familiar voice came echoing hollowly down the phone, bringing a tremor to her knees that shocked her deeply. She was over all that! Why did he still affect her like this?

'I'm fine, thanks. Very busy, but really well.' She was proud of the composure of her voice. Her legs might be shaking and her insides turned to jelly, but she doubted that he could possibly guess.

'Nothing new?'

What did he want to know? Why had he rung? Suspicion flared within her.

Whatever it was, she was damned if she would make it easy for him. Gone were the days when she poured out all her hopes and dreams and plans to this man.

'Nothing much,' she answered finally.

'Heard the Archangel has offered you a job.' His voice was nonchalant, but she knew immediately that this was why he was ringing. What did it have to do with Mark?

He must be finished his residency and, as far as she knew, would be going into private practice somewhere. The thoughts flashed through her head, her mind puzzling at this unexpected contact.

'I've done a few days in Theatre with him, but that's as far as it goes.' It was a half-truth. From the first hours in Theatre with him she had known that she would go—if she suited him!

He had not mentioned India since that first evening, and she was content to wait for his verdict.

'The thing is, darling——' how dared he call her that? she thought '—I've decided that I'd like to specialise in plastic surgery and, although I've done my primaries, I need to get on to the programme. The Archangel decides who's on and who's off, and I thought if you were working with him you might be able to put in a good word.'

'When did you decide to do this?' she asked, surprised by his decision. 'I thought general practice was the only reason you chose to study medicine. You always said you despised all those specialists, making themselves rich on taxpayers' money. If I remember rightly——' and I do, she told herself '—cosmetic surgery was your pet hate.'

Even as she repeated the words, she wondered if it was Mark's influence that had made her critical of the cosmetic cutters.

'I've been thinking of specialising for a while now. There's not much money in general practice these days.'

'Caroline wants a rich husband, does she?' The words were out before she could stop them. Far from feeling remorse at her bitchiness, she experienced a sense of relief that she could now accept the situation and treat it lightly.

'I'm not seeing Caroline any more,' he told her sharply. 'I thought you would have known that. I've always regretted what happened, Leith, and felt badly about the way I treated you.'

She heard the wheedling tones of a schoolboy that Mark had always used when he was late, or stood her up for one reason or another, a little boy looking for forgiveness, and certain that it would be forthcoming.

Today it had no effect on her, and she grinned to herself, suddenly conscious of a great victory in her life. She was free of Mark at last.

'I'm sorry, I can't help. I've only just met the man. I can hardly bob up in Theatre and say, "By the way, an old boyfriend of mine wants a job on your team". I'm sure if you're good enough you'll make it. Good luck, Mark, and thanks for calling.'

She hung up abruptly, then sat down, her legs suddenly weak. She would go to India if she 'suited' Gabe, go and enjoy it. She had cast off the past and, although there were shadows of yesterday that were not so easily discarded, she would be going into this great new adventure with a light heart and a confidence in herself that she'd thought had gone forever.

CHAPTER TWO

THE turbulent dreams that had troubled her since she accepted Gabe Vincent's proposition seemed destined to follow her to India. During the time she had spent in Theatre with him a reluctant respect for his ability had grown within her, but she was increasingly disturbed by her physical reaction to the man.

Accepting that it was simply part of a healing process that had been delayed for too long, she threw herself into work and the necessary preparations for her trip. There followed a month of hectic activity — organising a passport, visa, inoculations, finding someone to rent her house, and learning the ways of a new surgeon.

It left her pale and exhausted, and the sleep she had hoped to make up on the flight was tortured by the now familiar nightmares.

'Do you always twitch and moan in your sleep?' The enigmatic man with whom she travelled had woken her gently, to tell her they would soon be landing in Singapore.

His question confused her tired mind, and she looked questioningly at him. Her soft, shining hair tumbled around her face, and her sleep-dazed eyes widened with bewilderment as she fought to make sense of her surroundings.

Seeing her disorientation, he leaned forward and unlatched her seatbelt. He had moved a bare six inches, but the closeness of the seats brought him into contact

HEALING LOVE

with her body, and she felt again that unfamiliar surge of awareness of his maleness.

He was so close that she could see the faint track-like marks across his forehead, and the furrowed lines that a frown had imprinted between his straggly black brows.

His black hair seemed thick and strong, springing vigorously back from his brow, and she could detect the faintest whiff of shampoo and aftershave — the intimate male scents that she had missed for so long.

Bemused by the combination of sleep and his closeness, she continued her inspection. His top lip showed the shadow where his dark moustache would grow, and she could detect a slight stubble of prickly black hair on his chin. The dark swarthiness of unshaven skin contrasted strongly with his pale, pinkish lips, rimmed by a fine white line that seemed to sculpt them into a distinct feature that was part and yet not part of the whole.

A faint tremor shook her as her eyes feasted on those lips until, startled by her thoughts, she quickly lifted her eyes to his. Had he detected her interest? Apparently not, for he was gazing straight ahead, his attention fixed on a hostess who was handing out landing cards to passengers disembarking at Singapore.

They were really the most remarkable eyes she had ever seen, she thought as she continued her scrutiny. A deep blue, set well back beneath his black eyebrows, and fringed with long, dark lashes that would drive any woman mad with envy.

She sighed, confused by her physical response to this remote man. He had pressed himself back against his own seat, leaving her free to struggle past him to the bathroom.

She stepped over his long legs, and headed down the aisle between the rows of seats. In the cramped compartment she did what she could to repair the damage that an uneasy few hours of sleep had wrought, and to control the errant thoughts that had flitted through her tired mind.

He was all business when she returned—but when was he any different?

'I'll be going through Customs when we disembark, and they'll keep you in the transit lounge, so I'll give you the tickets for all the baggage.'

She had known he was staying in Singapore to organise surgical equipment, but this reminder brought a flutter of apprehension in the pit of her stomach. Sensing her unease, he spoke quickly to reassure her.

'Carew's representative, Noel Williams, will be at Madras airport to meet you, and he'll take care of all the gear. I've written down the number where I'm staying in case you need to contact me. If you could check the theatre to see if there's anything extra we'll need, and let me know before Friday, I'd be grateful.'

She nodded reluctant agreement, tucking the baggage tickets into her pocket. Her usual brisk efficiency deserted her momentarily.

'I'll see you Friday, then.'

'Don't sound so forlorn. This is supposed to be an adventure for you. I know we'll be working darned hard, but you must still enjoy yourself. Play the tourist for a few days, then you'll be able to show me all the sights when I arrive.'

She brightened at his words. Maybe he wasn't as cold and unapproachable as she had been picturing him.

'I've never travelled outside Australia before,' she

explained, suddenly able to confess the reason for her forebodings.

He turned to stare at her in amazement, his eyes crinkling into a sympathetic smile as he took in her woebegone face.

'Good heavens, girl, what are you working so hard for, if it isn't for the fun of spending the money you deservedly earn? I thought all young single women travelled compulsively these days.'

She shook her head, feeling her hair flick about her heated cheeks as she vehemently denied his assumptions.

'Not me; I've other plans for my money.'

She clutched her dream tightly to her, determination strengthened by his casual words.

Madras was an enthralling, intoxicating world of enchantment. From the time she moved out of the air-conditioned airport into the damp humidity of the Indian evening she was entranced by the wonder of it all. As Noel Williams led her to the company's small car she felt the velvety softness of the night close around her, aromatic with fragrances she could only identify as 'foreign'.

'It even smells different!' The words escaped her lips, although she was shamed by her naïveté.

'You can say that again. I've never known a place that smells this bad.' His American twang rang in her ears, and his abrupt disparagement tempered her delight.

'And the heat! It'll kill you, believe me!'

'Are you here permanently?' She was disconcerted by his obvious distaste for the place.

'No way. I see you people settled in, make sure

you're happy with the set-up, and I'm off. I've lived most parts of the world, but this place is not for Mrs Williams' little boy!'

As if the heat precluded further conversation, they drove in a deepening silence towards the city; the sculptured pyramids of temple towers, rising like dark shadows on the skyline, promised Leith a feast of rich visual delights in the days to come.

'Where's Williams?' It was some days later that Gabe Vincent emerged from Customs, looking tired and dishevelled, his dark hair lank with sweat and a prickly stubble shadowing his face.

'I've sent him home. He hates India.' She grinned at him as she spoke, unaware of the radiance that her excitement lent to her pretty face.

'And you don't?'

'Oh, Dr Vincent, I would never have believed that a place could be so wonderful. It throbs and shimmers and sparkles.'

'You're doing a bit of shimmering and sparkling yourself,' he remarked with an amused indulgence, 'and I thought we'd reached first-name terms. It's Gabe, remember.'

'Yes, well. . .' She was suddenly shy. All the enthusiasm of her love-affair for the fascinating city evaporated as she stood beside him, embarrassed by the colour of her language and the unexpected spurt of happiness she had felt on seeing him.

'Lead me to the car and you can tell me all about it as we drive into the city.'

'You're probably more interested in the theatre and hospital than my sightseeing. It's just that I find it so overwhelming, all my impressions keep wanting to burst out.'

'Don't feel embarrassed about enthusiasm, Leith.' His deep voice washed over her. 'There's nothing worse than the blasé traveller who feels obliged to be bored by all he or she sees.'

'Well, I'll start with the theatre anyway. Here's the car.'

'Where's the driver? Did we miss him on the way?'

'I'm the driver,' she teased. 'Scared?'

'You have settled in!' He grinned at her as she opened the doors and helped him stow his luggage in the back seat.

She concentrated on getting out of the car park and back on to the main road that she now knew so well. The silence between them was comfortable, and the night wove its customary magic about her.

'Reminds me of nights at home when I was a kid,' he said, breathing deeply as they drove through the humid darkness.

'The spicy, fragrant air?'

'Not that so much as the feel of the tropical night, wrapping around one like a damp blanket. The air at home smelled sweet—sickly sweet to strangers, but not to us kids. It's the smell of money, my dad would say.'

'Where was this?' She asked the question quietly, not wanting to spoil his train of thought, to halt his reminiscence.

'North Queensland,' he replied, turning to look at a temple that had loomed up beside the car. 'My family had a cane farm. Italians opened up the cane fields in the north.'

'It's quite a jump, from cane farming to plastic surgery.'

A soft sigh caught her ears before he replied, 'A lot bigger jump than anyone could imagine. Sometimes. . .' His voice trailed away and she wondered what he'd been about to say. 'Enough of this,' he changed the subject abruptly, and she knew she'd never know! 'How's our theatre?'

'It's great. You probably know that it's a mobile army type of thing that can be set up anywhere.'

'Yes, I've seen them on display, and the company sent a brochure.'

He seemed to relax as they went along, and now turned from the sights they were passing to fix his eyes on her as she drove.

'It's an anomaly, isn't it?' he muttered with an audible regret. 'We send young men out to get shot, then fly in a complete operating-theatre and hospital to patch them up again.'

'So that they can go back to the war.' The thought sobered her, tempering her delight in their new workplace.

A silence fell between them as they both contemplated the ironies of war. It was Gabe who broke it, seeing the positive benefits that something so devastating could produce.

'I suppose we must remember that many things are invented for war that have far-reaching effects in peacetime. If this theatre is as revolutionary as they say it is, I have some ideas of my own for its future use.'

'It's fantastic,' she told him eagerly. 'So compact, yet efficient. There's an ante-room, a small scrub-room — or alcove, really — and a recovery-room. The local people here have made a passage from there to the old house that will be used as a hospital.'

HEALING LOVE

'We're not attached to a hospital?' She heard the astonishment in his voice.

'No. It seems that it would put too much pressure on the system, so they've been training nurses specially to handle our cases and have seconded them to us. I've met most of the girls, and I know it will work.'

'What kind of a place did they find to accommodate all our patients, not to mention nurses, kitchens, a laundry and all the other paraphernalia of a hospital?' he asked, mystified by this development.

She grinned in the darkness.

'Did you know that Southern India has a large Catholic population?'

'As it happens, I did, but what's that got to do with our hospital?'

'Just that it's a nunnery—or was. It's perfect—all the patients will have private rooms.'

'I suppose the authorities know what they're doing. Where are we now?'

'This is your hotel.'

An immaculately uniformed, turbaned Sikh appeared and opened the door of the small, grubby car, but Gabe Vincent ignored him.

'*My* hotel? And where are you staying?'

'At the nunnery, of course.'

'Of all the. . .'

She chuckled cheekily at his astonished reaction, but allowed him no time to argue. 'I'll drive over and collect you in the morning. Eight o'clock too early?'

'The efficient Sister Robinson! No, eight o'clock will not be too early, and you'll have some explaining to do.' He closed the car door and followed his baggage into the hotel.

Leith watched the broad back disappear from view

and sighed contentedly. So far so good, she thought to herself, admitting to a certain pleasurable feeling now that a familiar figure was here to share her adventure. Was it just the presence of someone from home that warmed her?

He was an unusually attractive man—not classically handsome, for his features were too strongly defined for that, but there was something. . . She shrugged aside these fancies—better not to follow that line of thought!

Her body reacted to some chemical charges that emanated from his well-knit frame. She could admit that much—but her life was mapped out, and her plans did not include a man, however attractive or chemically appealing.

'And his life would certainly not include you, Leith Robinson.' She spoke the words aloud, chastising herself for allowing her mind to rove into the realms of fantasy. She had learned to keep the sadness at bay and to still the longing of her body for a man's touch. She must think instead of the certain future, the one she had determined, and that destiny could not touch.

'The hospital is in the suburb of Mylapore, at the other end of this long beach.' She had been waiting when he came out of the hotel, crisply cool in an open-necked white shirt and shorts.

'Now that is a beach!' he exclaimed with a certain wonder as they drove on to the esplanade.

The wide white sands had their usual clutter of people. Far out, beyond the massive ocean waves, crescent-shaped fishing boats bobbed on the horizon as they swung coloured nets from their bows.

'It's magnificent, isn't it? But it's not used the way we use our beaches at home.'

'No swimmers and sunbathers?'

'Only a few foreign tourists ever swim. The locals say there are undercurrents that tow you out, and hungry sharks, but I think it's just the different culture. Certainly no Indian would want more colour from the sun, particularly here in the South, where lightness of skin is highly regarded.'

Even with her eyes fixed on the medley of bicycles, cattle, people and old vehicles that made driving in India so hazardous she was aware of a quizzical smile on his face as he teased her indulgently.

'You've picked up plenty of local knowledge in a few days.'

'I know,' she apologised quickly. 'I'll bore you to tears. Just tell me to stop when you get tired of it. It's all so new and exciting, somehow.'

'Don't clam up on me now. I'm still waiting to hear what they do with so much beach.'

They had reached the end of the esplanade by now and were turning towards the hospital.

'You'll see. This evening, when you go back to the hotel, there'll be thousands of people—a sort of milling, brightly coloured throng—walking along the sands to take in the cool sea breeze after the humidity of the day. It's an amazing sight. And then there's the mornings. . .'

She broke off and smiled, recollecting the magic of her first morning in this so foreign city.

'I can't tell you about the mornings. It's something that everyone has to see for themselves. Here we are.'

The drab camouflage canvas of the hospital tent stuck out like a growth on the side of a lovely old building. Leith swung the car into the deep shade of a large rain tree, and led him towards the front of the low-set building.

'We can't get into the theatre from outside. It seemed best to keep it completely sealed off because of the dust and flies.'

'Do we slit the walls with a scalpel, in case of an emergency exit?'

She laughed at his words.

'Something like that,' she replied, pleased that he seemed so human and approachable in this different setting.

The wide, red-tiled veranda looked cool and inviting after the short walk across the dusty yard, and a small-boned young woman stood ready to receive them at the front door.

'This is Kala Ambedkar, Dr Vincent. She's in charge of the hospital and nursing staff.'

A sweet smile of welcome lit up Kala's face as she asked hopefully, 'We can start today?'

Leith watched the man expectantly, knowing that he was perceptive enough to catch the eagerness in Kala's soft voice.

'In a hurry, are we, girls?' He smiled at them. 'Do we have the patients?'

Silently the two women turned and led him to the side-veranda, where about thirty people squatted patiently on their haunches.

'They've been here since the theatre tent was put up, Gabe.' Leith spoke quietly. 'They disappear at night, but first thing in the morning they're back.'

She watched his eyes scan the waiting people, taking in the bulging, shiny pink scars and puckered red distortions left by the burns. The sight had sickened

Leith on her first day, but she now saw past the disfigurement, and was slowly befriending the people who sat there each day.

'These people were the lucky ones,' said Leith. 'I've seen those who were inside the actual factory, and the damage to their limbs was ghastly. At least the office workers still have the use of their hands, even if their faces are mutilated and scarred.'

'Don't you believe that physical appearance is important to these people? Don't you understand the inner torment they must suffer, having to face the world with such grotesque masks where their faces used to be?'

He thrust the words angrily at her, so that his quiet fury had a physical reaction, and she flinched back from him.

'We'll start today, Sister,' he continued coldly. 'Get hold of Dr Prakash and the anaesthetist. I have the doctor's case-notes and will take the patients in the order he suggests. Do you have the lists?'

He turned to Leith again.

'Yes, sir.'

Her training took over, and she fell into the formality of their professional roles with relief, the hurt his earlier words had caused banished by the immediacy of the new situation.

'They follow Dr Prakash's case-notes almost exactly.'

'Very well. Sister Ambedkar, if you would have your staff prep the first patient while I check out the theatre and Sister Robinson sets up, we'll get this show on the road.'

A low murmur of approval rose from the waiting throng, and a shifting of bodies signalled an awareness that their patience would soon be rewarded.

* * *

The throb of the air-conditioning motor dropped to a low hum, indicating that the thermostat was cutting back as the air cooled outside. It was the only indication that day was drawing towards evening. Leith wiggled her toes inside her shoes and shifted her weight imperceptibly from one foot to another.

'I'm glad you included this chap among the first lot, Prakash. He'll only need a simple excision to remove all that scar tissue, then some fancy stitching to mask the new scar. Z or W would you say, Sister?'

'Zplasty,' she answered promptly, then caught the surprise in Gabe's blue eyes, and her own twinkled back at him.

'It's a guess,' she admitted. 'I know you removed a scar on that first day I was in Theatre with you, and you explained how you cut a pattern in the skin to make the edges less defined, but the finer points of it all escaped me!'

'It was a good guess. It's exactly what we will do. See, Prakash, I mark where I'm going to cut with methylene blue, because it's easier to change blue marks than it is to change a scalpel incision. You probably use a similar marker in your surgery.'

'Following the contours of the face?'

'That's right.' His fingers handled the scalpel with a delicate expertise. 'The doctors who were trying to save these people's lives had no time for fancy work. Their main aim would have been to get the wound covered to stop further loss of fluid and prevent infection. Now that the scars have settled we will be able to pretty things up quite a bit. It will encourage the others when they see what we can do.'

Gabe's hands moved surely as he spoke, his white-capped head bent low over the operating-table. Leith heard the assistant's murmur of agreement and saw the pleasure in his liquid brown eyes as he nodded his acknowledgement.

'So many will need three, four operations, in spite of what we have been able to do in preparation. It will be good for them to see this man made better in a shorter time, give everyone hope.

'Your preparations have been excellent, from what I've seen so far. My job is the easy one.' His deep voice was muffled by his mask, but there was genuine admiration in Gabe's words.

'It may be easy to you,' Prakash said, as he watched gloved fingers move with incredible speed and precision, securing the serrated edges of the wound together with microscopic stitches. 'We have surgeons with the skill, but not as much expertise. It is good that I learn from you. I can pass on to my colleagues and students some of your methods. Microsurgery is still fairly rare in this country. The facilities are located in some major cities, and smaller towns must wait.'

'I can't imagine there being much call for cosmetic surgery in India.' Even as the words left her lips, Leith regretted them. What had made her say something so stupid, so likely to raise Gabe's anger?

For the second time that day, those blue eyes flashed irritably at her. His scowl of contempt was intensified by the framing of his white mask and cap, so that she had the same feeling as an unwanted visitor, viewed through a slit in a door.

'Sister Robinson sees all cosmetic surgery as an expression of vanity. She prefers to be involved in more useful miracles like the restoration of sight.'

She opened her lips to protest, but was not quick

enough to defend herself, as Prakash took on the role of instructor.

'Cosmetic surgery is a very old custom in this country, Sister,' he explained, in his soft, melodious voice. 'Our history shows doctors doing this many centuries ago. Not as well as Dr Vincent, of course.'

Surprised by this knowledge, Leith bent her head over her tray, fiddling quietly with the remaining instruments. Mentally she accepted Gabe's criticism and resolved to watch her wayward tongue in future.

Was it the constant argument about the value of different specialities that she heard in the day hospital that had given her a bias against this type of work, or was it Mark's influence?

Both things, she decided, plus her own horror when she had heard of Katherine's beautiful face being carved up for vanity—his, she had no doubt!

'If you've finished sulking, Sister, I'll have that non-adhesive dressing, and we can get out of here.'

Gabe's voice brought her back to the present, and she lifted mutinous eyes to glare at him over her mask, before settling the gauze into place and starting the bandage that would hold it firm. The long day had nearly ended.

'Prakash will drop me back at the hotel. See you get plenty of sleep; it's been a long day.' He spoke brusquely, stripping off his gloves and gown.

'You can take the car, if you like. Then you'll be independent,' she told him, wanting to cut off personal contact between herself and this antagonistic man.

'It's probably pitch-dark outside, and I doubt if I'd find the way. Do you mind collecting me at the hotel again in the morning?'

She could hear exhaustion in his voice, and instantly

regretted her hasty remark that had killed the tentative rapport that was growing between them.

'I'll leave the car outside your hotel in the morning and give the keys to the receptionist. If you follow the beach back to here you won't get lost.'

'And how will you get back?'

'I'll walk. I walk on the beach each morning.' The intense joy this activity brought to her lightened her voice, as if anticipating the pleasure was nearly as good as experiencing it.

'Indeed? Maybe I'll join you.' With that surprising riposte Gabriel Vincent, known as the Archangel, turned on his heel and walked out of the room.

She moved away to collect the instruments and follow the scrub nurse to the sink where everything had to be washed before being replaced on the trays and stacked in the steriliser. After explaining what she wanted, Leith returned to the theatre.

Leaving the bright lights burning, she washed down all the dull metal surfaces and set out sterile packs on the trolley, ready for the following day. She worked automatically, following the routine that she had used for years, her mind free to wander back over the long day.

After mentally ticking off the patients she would have to check on before she went to bed, her mind strayed to the cool and competent surgeon, who had come so far to offer hope to these people.

She believed him when he told her that he was doing it for the money. There had been an eagerness in his voice when he mentioned it that confirmed his words. It puzzled her that a man whose sole aim was so mercenary would care about these people. That he did care, and care deeply, was equally obvious!

The ambiguity of it all still teased at her mind much later as she was drifting off to sleep. Then the man she kept glimpsing behind the façade appeared in some nebulous fantasy that carried her into oblivion.

CHAPTER THREE

GABE was sitting on the steps of the hotel like a flesh-and-blood copy of Rodin's *Thinker* when she drove up in the shadowy darkness that preceded the swift tropical dawn.

'I'll leave the keys with the doorman. He'll park it away somewhere,' he greeted her as he moved to open the car door.

He swung a light day-pack on to his back and, after throwing the keys neatly to the attendant, fell into step beside her. She was above average height, but he still topped her by a head, she thought, as she mentally measured herself against him.

'It's about an eight-kilometre walk,' she said guardedly, disturbed by his presence. She did not know him well enough to gauge his moods, but instinct prompted her to tread warily.

'Think I won't make it?' He grinned at her, the simple rearrangement of facial muscles brightening his saturnine face.

His eyes rested on her face, free of make-up, and lightly tanned after her days of sightseeing. She could almost feel his gaze as it settled on her eyes, liquid brown meeting deepest blue, then travelled down to rest on her well-shaped mouth.

He seemed to nod as if confirming some inner thought, before smiling again as his eyes continued their inspection, taking in her unconventional attire.

'Is this normal walking gear in India, Sister Robinson? Will I be over-dressed on your beach?'

Leith coloured under his gentle raillery as she glanced down at her bright pink silk trousers that ballooned out from a narrow waist to tight bands around her ankles. Teamed with a pale pink T-shirt bearing the words 'Run for Your Life', it was hardly high fashion!

'I did bring jogging gear with me,' she explained, 'but Indian women are so modest, I felt it would be distasteful of me to parade my legs on their beach. I found these trousers in the market, and they're light and surprisingly cool.'

His intent appraisal had disconcerted her, and she rushed into further speech.

'It's strange how people of European stock bare their bodies in the heat, while people who live in the very hot climates cover up for coolness.'

She kept chattering as she led the way down the short lane to the beach, as much from nervousness as a desire to talk.

'You seem to have become very sensitive to the local feelings and customs,' was the grave response. 'Perhaps, in time, you will become equally sensitive to mine.'

She spun around to face him, dismayed that he should still be holding her hasty words against her, but the wry grin that twisted his finely moulded lips told her that he was teasing.

'I'm sorry if I seemed critical last night,' she said contritely. 'Sometimes I open my mouth and silly things come out.'

'Apology accepted. Is this your beach?'

The lane had opened on to the top of a low dune,

and before them, nearly half a kilometre wide, stretched the sand.

Above the high-tide mark, its softness was pockmarked by the thousands of feet that had walked on it the previous evening. Below this meandering line it lay smooth, gleaming dully as it stretched to meet the foaming waves.

In the indistinct light they could see the shadows of cattle being washed in the shallows, then a brilliant flush lit up the eastern sky and curtains of colour hung suspended, turning the wet sand into a shining sheet of red and gold. The flaming ball of the sun rose majestically from the sea, a grand entrance for the leading character.

Leith held her breath. It was a miracle she had witnessed several times now, but it never failed to thrill her.

'I can see why you walk. Shall we go, or will mere mortals like us spoil the magic?' He murmured the words, caught in the spell of that moment of sheer and radiant beauty.

She walked swiftly now, across the wide beach towards the water's edge, breathing deeply to suck in the fresh, tangy air.

'At home I walk for exercise. Here it's for sheer pleasure. To me it's like a magic show repeated every morning. Not only the gaudy opening with the sunrise, but the unfamiliar rituals that people are performing as part of a way of life that has been followed for centuries.'

She waved a hand towards a loincloth-clad figure, standing on one leg in the shallow wash of the waves, his arms raised and twisted above his head in a pose more familiar to a temple statue.

'I presume the people on the dry sand are sleeping rather than dead?' He asked the question quietly, bending close to her ear, his nearness disturbing in a way that she did not want to analyse.

'I think they sleep out here because it is cooler, rather than because they have no homes. Kala tells me that poverty and homelessness are not bad in Madras. People cram into the big cities like Bombay and Delhi when they are destitute.'

'You're certainly a mine of information in a short time! Now perhaps while we are walking you will tell me why you are staying at the hospital, not at the hotel. Saving your expenses money?'

She blushed at his words, but defended her decision.

'Only partly that.'

'And partly what else? Honestly, Leith Robinson, getting personal information out of you is like drawing teeth. You're definitely not the chattiest of theatre sisters I've ever worked with.'

She laughed at his observation, aware that her reserve was a protective instinct, and determined to keep it intact. Work was the one subject she felt safe discussing, so she tried to make him understand the reasons for her decision.

'I spent some time with the sister who usually specials your patients before I came over, because I was concerned about care after the operation.'

'You won't have to worry about that. India does have competent nurses.'

She ignored the irony in his voice, still anxious to get her point across.

'I know I'm not responsible for post-operative care, but it's a long time since I did general nursing duties, and things change all the time. I wanted to know what techniques were used to ensure the best chance of success.'

The words came out in a rush, embarrassment again causing her to explain too much, too quickly.

'Don't sound so defensive about it, Leith. It's a very admirable trait to be so thorough in your preparations for a job, but it still doesn't explain your living in at the hospital.'

'Well. . .' How to explain without sounding patronising, without belittling the professionalism of the women she was coming to know and admire?

'The nurses here are about at the level I was at before Margaret brought me up to date. I thought if I was on hand I could show them a few things, and help them get it right. I can also check that the theatre is properly cleaned each evening.'

She sought her words with care.

'It's not that I don't trust the staff; I just like to check things for myself. They had spare rooms, and I pay board. You don't mind, do you?'

'It's none of my business where you stay,' he answered curtly, 'but see that you don't get so involved that your work in the theatre suffers. You will be putting in long hours there, and I need you to be on the ball.'

He had withdrawn from her again, wrapping himself in an almost palpable screen of indifference, and cutting off the pleasant human being that she glimpsed from time to time.

They walked in silence, watching fishermen launch their catamarans, fighting through the breaking surf to the rolling swells of the deep water beyond the breakers.

The sleepers struggled back to life. Like an army of

ants they rose, rolled up their mats, and trudged towards the esplanade. The cattle, glistening wet, obeyed their masters' prods, and headed towards their daily duties.

'I keep misjudging you.'

His harshly muttered admission broke into her thoughts.

'I beg your pardon?'

He paused and reached out a hand to take her arm and turn her to face him. She felt again the sudden flare of awareness that his touch had evoked on the plane, and wondered if he felt the tremors that flickered and fluttered through her body. His back was towards the now burning sun, and his face was dark with shadows.

'I don't usually make snap judgements about people, but I seem to have done this with you. You keep throwing me completely off balance, and the only way I can explain that is by accepting that I must have had some preconceived ideas about you.'

She recognised a desperation in his words, as if he was battling some inner force. Anxious to protect her own carefully constructed reserve, she resolved to treat his words with a lightness they probably did not deserve.

'"Money-hungry" being chief among them?'

'You put yourself down too easily, Leith. You show people the sides of yourself that you want them to accept as the real thing, and keep your other self hidden from prying eyes. I wonder why?'

The words were the quiet reflections of a man speaking his thoughts aloud.

If he didn't know, he must be the only medical person in the whole of south-east Queensland who had missed the gossip, Leith thought, with a sharp bitterness that she had not felt since her arrival in this mesmeric country.

'Don't we all project the image of ourselves that we want others to accept?'

'To a certain extent, I suppose,' he agreed thoughtfully, 'but most people show the world their best side.'

They had turned again and were walking slowly, the eddying tide of people and animals now passing unnoticed.

'That's a gross generalisation, Dr Vincent, and all this philosophy is too much before breakfast.' She laughed with a false gaiety. 'We leave the beach here.'

In spite of her flippant words, Leith shivered as she turned away from the sparkling water.

She had a sudden presentiment that this man, whose lightest touch could provoke an involuntary physical reaction within her, could peel away the layers of her composure as easily as he shaved skin off his patients for their grafts.

'Did you read through the list Prakash suggested for today?'

So his mind had switched back to their work, she thought, and allowed hers to follow gratefully.

'Yes, I know Anani, who's listed first. She's been one of those who waited each day on the veranda. Waiting for a miracle,' she added almost inaudibly, intending the words only for herself.

'Listen to you!' he mocked. 'You don't sound at all like the cool, impersonal, efficient theatre sister you pretend to be when you talk about a case like that!'

'Oh, Gabe! She's so young, and was obviously beautiful before that fireball swept past her face.' All the anguish that she felt was revealed in her words.

Anani, with her shy smile and gentle patience, was a favourite with everyone at the hospital, but was especially dear to Leith.

The shock that she had felt when she first saw the terrible scars disfiguring one side of that perfect face was still vivid in her mind, and she shuddered at the horror that the young girl had endured. It was as if a malevolent puppet maker had created a face that would shock his audience to the core—with a serene beauty on one half of the puppet's head, and a twisted abhorrence on the other.

'We can't perform miracles, Leith,' Gabe said with tender consideration. His arm wrapped around her shoulders in a gesture of sympathy as he saw the sadness in her soft eyes. 'But we can improve things greatly.'

'Yes?' she queried doubtfully, warmed by his empathy with her concern.

'Yes,' he said, so positively that she had to believe him. His arm tightened about her, then he turned to face her, holding her shoulders with his strong hands, and looking directly into her eyes.

'Believe me! It will take more than one operation, but Anani will smile again and blink again and, with the help of some clever camouflage make-up, will be willing to look at herself in the mirror once again.'

'Oh, Gabe!' She breathed his name, grateful for his reassurance, but with thoughts of Anani slipping from her mind as his beautiful eyes met hers with a message that she could not read.

The still figure cloaked in white had lost the identity of the gentle girl, and become another 'case'. The anaesthetist's paraphernalia hummed, and the muffled shuffling of clumsy theatre slippers provided a descant to the clinking of instruments and muted requests.

Leith moved with her usual automatic efficiency, aiming always to anticipate the surgeons' needs, while constantly checking on the other activities in the theatre.

Gabe had surveyed the puckered scars in silence, then marked an area that stretched from in front of Anani's left ear to the corner of her mouth. With consummate skill he applied the small machine he used for dermabrasion — a technique more common in the wealthy suburbs of Western society than here in the south of India. It removed layers of ageing skin, or, in this case, layers of graft and scarring.

Having assisted him in this procedure before, Leith kept the area irrigated efficiently while Prakash cleared the débrided tissue as they prepared a viable bleeding bed to receive the graft.

Using saline-soaked pads, Leith kept the site moist, applying a gentle pressure to prevent haemorrhage, and lifting the dressings clear as Gabe measured the wound he wanted to cover.

'Try the template!'

She removed the pads as Prakash fitted the aluminium sheet, cut to shape over the area to be covered.

A little adjustment and they were right, with a perfect pattern for the piece of skin that would be fitted over the girl's cheek.

As the two men moved away again Leith continued her mopping operations.

She was well aware of the ever present problem that the blood-vessels caused. It was essential to have a good supply of blood to the site to promote the acceptance of the foreign skin, but there was danger in excessive bleeding that could lead to the development of a thrombosis and the ultimate rejection of the graft.

'Good girl!'

Gabe's quiet encouragement sent a tiny spurt of happiness through her as she watched him lift the dressings.

'We'll need a large, full-thickness sheet to cover the cheek, Prakash.'

'From her neck, then.' The Indian doctor was confident in his knowledge, and indicated an area that he had already marked above her fragile clavicle.

'I think so,' Gabe replied, 'although we'll leave another scar there.'

'Her hair will hide it eventually,' Leith murmured, and looked up to see Gabe wink at her, his eyes twinkling delightedly.

'I've never said that we can't *try* to make people look as good as possible,' she responded defensively.

'Just that it was slightly amoral for a man to earn his money doing it?' he teased, before turning back to his fellow surgeon.

'The donor site will be too big to heal successfully without help,' he continued, the statement intimating a question.

He constantly encouraged Prakash to make decisions, and already Leith could see the younger surgeon growing in confidence. He's a kind man, she thought irrelevantly, sneaking a glance at him from over her mask.

'I thought that might be the case, Gabe, so we've prepped an area on her leg. We can take a small, split-thickness sheet from there and mesh it to cover the area we'll need.'

Leith lifted the tray of dermatomes. They were small

machines that the surgeons used to shave the millimetres of good skin they needed for grafts. She passed it towards Gabe, who selected the size and width he wanted before nodding towards Prakash.

They prepared to work simultaneously, Gabe adjusting the manually operated instrument to the desired thickness, while Prakash applied sterile mineral oil to the site.

Leith's eyes followed the strong, sure fingers of the surgeon as he moved the drum of the dermatome smoothly across the undamaged skin, shaving off the fine layer required for this first stage of their work.

She handed Gabe the tray and he took the skin to his work trolley, where he cut it with precision to match the template. Meanwhile Prakash had selected another dermatome and indicated to her to prepare the site on the girl's leg with mineral oil as he began to take an even finer layer of skin from there.

'Have you meshed skin before?' she murmured quietly to Kala, aware that speed was essential at this stage of the operation.

Kala shook her head, her eyes doubtful about some new responsibility being thrust upon her.

'That's OK. Swap places, and you stand by here for Gabe and I'll do the mesh.'

She held the small tool towards Prakash, and watched as he placed the harvested skin on the carriers and checked that it was the right way up.

Turning the handle slowly, she checked as the carrier rolled through the mesher, cutting small holes in the skin to allow it to be stretched to cover a larger area.

'I'd normally close with staples, but her skin is so damaged, I think sutures will hold better.' Gabe had the sheet of skin in place over the prepared area.

Leith passed the carrier to Prakash, and moved back to her place opposite Gabe to pass him the first of the needle holders, with the finest of threads barely visible. She turned the magnifying light towards him and unconsciously held her breath as she watched him stitch the patch into place. The silence in the small, womb-like room stretched to an almost unbearable tension before Gabe finally knotted the last suture.

'There!' he muttered, raising his head with a satisfied sigh, before concentrating once more as he covered the entire site with a fine gauze dressing and taped it lightly in place.

A collective exhalation of breath echoed his as the watchers relaxed once again and the normal routines of the theatre took over.

'I'll leave you to close that donor site with the meshed skin, Prakash, and Leith can dress the wound on her leg. I'll check on yesterday's patients in the interval, see if any nasty little problems are lurking in the wounds.'

Leith watched him leave the theatre, and, in a rare moment of inattention, allowed her thoughts to wander back to their morning walk along the beach.

'I'll use those steri-strips to hold this in place, thanks, Leith.' Prakash's voice brought her back to reality, and she quickly found him the necessary closures from the orderly arrangement on her tray. 'And we'll use Bioprane dressings on the donor site and this meshed graft.'

Dragging her mind back to the present, Leith inwardly rebuked herself. Not since the first heady days of her romance with Mark had she ever allowed her attention to wander while she was in Theatre. Why was this happening now?

The same procedures were repeated, with infinite variations, throughout the day, as they worked with steady assurance to minimise the damage of the dreadful explosion. Leith was amazed by the complexity of what had seemed such a simple speciality.

The surgeons conferred endlessly, discussing the viability of such a graft for such a site, what skin would most easily replace an eyelid, and which would most nearly replicate the whorling curves of an ear.

As each new graft was successfully anchored into place one or other of the men would leave the theatre to check on post-operative patients and examine the healing wounds from the previous day.

'We need an extra pair of hands in this team,' Gabe said quietly as the last patient was wheeled out of the theatre. He was slumped against the instrument chest, his voice echoing slightly in the strange room. As he peeled off his mask Leith could see the lines of strain etched deeply down his cheeks, drawing his mouth into a grimace that told of his weariness.

'You need a break between patients, Gabe,' she protested. 'Can't you rethink this mad schedule of yours and do a little less each day?'

'Think of the money,' he taunted her tiredly, but she refused to be diverted.

'So we stay an extra month, and earn a little less. What the hell?' Her own exhaustion lent an edge to her voice—her day was far from over!

'And will you tell those people waiting out there that they'll have to wait even longer?' Gabe's voice held a hint of menace as he challenged her. 'Some of them need three operations, with a minimum of a week between them!'

'It's not so much the theatre work as the post-operative stuff. If we had someone to take that over, or relieve one of us in the theatre while we did it from time to time, it would all work extremely well,' Prakash cut in quickly, defusing the situation with his quiet good sense. Gabe looked hopefully at him.

'Any hope of digging up such a person, Prakash?'

'I'm afraid not. Our authorities are already annoyed that the damage caused by the foreign company has tied up their facilities for so long. Any mention of Carew's could start riots in the streets.'

He threw up his hands in a comical gesture of horror. 'There are many young graduates wishing to do further studies who would welcome the chance to work with you, but they are afraid to upset the Government. They might lose opportunities in the future.'

'But that's unfair! Indian people are in need of treatment; surely their own doctors should be permitted to provide it.'

'You are right, Leith, of course, but the Government has already provided my services, and the building, and other staff. Should they really have to do more?'

He spoke so quietly that Leith had to strain to hear him, and as she realised the full import of his words she felt a hot flush of shame sweep through her body. Did he know how much she and Gabe were earning? Compared to his salary, at local wages, it would seem like a fortune.

She shook her head as if to banish the disturbing thoughts, her eyes focused on the floppy slippers still tied to her feet.

'No, but you've given me an idea!'

She looked up at Gabe in astonishment, and noticed that Prakash was also watching with dubious eyes.

'Students!' said Gabe excitedly. 'Why didn't I think

of that before? You're a genius, Prakash. A few phone calls and *voilà*! I shall produce for you not a rabbit, but an extra pair of hands.'

Leith chuckled as she watched the bewilderment spread across the face of the local man. She hadn't followed Gabe's excited concept, but she understood the imagery he used, and was certain that he would make his idea work.

She watched him move towards Prakash and slip an arm around the other man's shoulders as he bent his head to explain as they walked from the theatre together.

Shrugging off the absurd pang of disappointment she felt as he disappeared without a backward glance, she set to work, organising the other nurses and aides as they scrubbed down the theatre and prepared to set up for the day ahead.

It was another two hours before she finished. Heading for the panelled dining-room, she swallowed a hasty meal, too weary to appreciate the tasty delicacies that had been served up to tempt her appetite. Her mind was still on her work as she walked down the long corridor that led past the patients' rooms to her own little 'cell' at the end of the building.

'Excuse me!'

A slight figure in an exquisite sari of peacock-blue emerged from one of the small rooms and called to her. Leith looked down to see Anani's mother grasping anxiously at her arm.

'I must leave now. It is the rules, but Anani. . .' The woman was visibly upset, and the hand that held Leith trembled slightly.

'She'll be all right,' Leith reassured her. 'The nurses

will watch her in case she wakes up in pain. I know she'll be well looked after.'

Thin dark fingers plucked feverishly at her arm, and Leith felt that it was fear more than anxiety that worried the older woman.

'She will wake with no one there!'

There was an edge of hysteria in the words, and Leith could see the strain in the woman's thin face and a kind of panic in her huge brown eyes, framed so dramatically by the gold-patterned border of the beautiful silk.

'I'll sit with her until she wakes.'

She heard her voice saying the words without conscious thought, and she patted the hand that lay on her arm.

'You go home now and rest, and in the morning you'll see for yourself just how much better she is!'

'You do so much for our people,' the woman murmured with gratitude, and raised her head to smile shyly at Leith, the worried lines in her face smoothing magically away.

'Thank you,' she added, and her sari-covered head bowed over joined hands in the traditional *namaste*, and Leith felt a lightness of spirit invade her weary body as she slipped through the open door to sit by Anani's bed.

Loose bandages swathed the small head, protecting the dressings over the new wounds. The visible parts of her face looked peaceful and her breathing was easy.

How much could they do? she wondered.

Her contemptuous rejection of cosmetic surgery in the past meant that she had studied very little about its success rates.

During her training she had seen patients recovering

from grafts, but the results had always seemed quite hideous—at least when they left the hospital.

The scars would lose their angry redness within a few weeks, and she thought most visible scars would eventually fade significantly, but how much better would the end results be?

Her eyes lingered on the beautiful skin on the undamaged side of Anani's face, and compassion for the young girl wrenched at her stomach.

The lovely girl was on the threshold of womanhood, yet would she ever know all the joys of being a woman? Would a man still love her? Would he see past that surface mutilation and love the person, not the face?

Even as the thoughts formed themselves in her mind, she realised that she was projecting a new despair of her own on to Anani—comparing their scars and their futures!

During the last twelve months she had built up an image of her own future—an image that excluded a close and loving relationship with any man.

By banning men from her dream she was insuring herself against further rejection and pain. After Mark's careless words it had been easier to believe in a rich and fulfilling life that centred around her career, and the secret dream of a child—a dream that she worked for and cherished.

Why, then, was she aching for Anani, aching because Anani might never know a man's love? Couldn't this young woman, lying so still before her, also have a satisfying life without a man?

'I'm too tired and too confused for all this soul-searching,' she told the sleeping figure on the bed. 'Perhaps I'll just hope that Gabe Vincent is as good as he thinks he is and your future will not be the lonely one I seem to be visualising!'

She shook herself crossly, annoyed by the unsettling images that were rattling her carefully constructed reserve.

A soft creak signalled the opening of the door behind her, and Leith turned, expecting to see one of the nurses entering to check on their charge.

But it was Gabe who stood there, blocking the light from the passage with his solid frame, and a twisting lurch in the region of her stomach confirmed Leith's forebodings.

It was Gabe Vincent who was ruffling the calm waters of her life. The potent attraction of his body to hers was clouding her judgement and disrupting her dreams.

'I heard you were here. Anani's mother spoke to me, and I've arranged for a nurse to sit with Anani until she wakes.'

'Why is she so concerned, Gabe?'

Leith whispered the question, partly out of concern for the sleeping girl, but his presence in that small, close room was so overwhelming that she doubted she could have found breath for a louder conversation.

He reached out a hand and drew her to her feet, leading her out into the corridor. One hand still held hers, firm and strong, and somehow very familiar, while his other hand came up to clasp her arm, so that they stood in a close intimacy in the quiet, sleeping night.

It seemed a long time before Gabe sighed deeply, then spoke with gentle care.

'It seems Anani has tried to kill herself several times.

It started after she came out of hospital the first time. Now her mother fears it may happen again.'

His fingers tightened on hers as the shock sent a tremor through her body. She felt a deadly coldness seeping through her veins, so that she shivered in the tepid night air.

'I'll make sure she's watched, Leith. We won't let that happen.'

He drew her close against his chest and she rested gratefully against him, drawing his warmth into her.

'If that's what she wants, are we wrong to stop her?' she pleaded, all the doubts she felt flooding back. 'What will the future hold for her? I've been thinking about it in there, Gabe!'

'Afraid of the future, Sister Robinson?' he taunted, pushing her away from his body and looking down into her eyes. 'You're over-tired and fanciful, little one, or you wouldn't be saying these things.'

He shook her slightly, as if to emphasise his point.

'It's not having a future to envisage that's the really frightening thing,' he said soberly. 'Just think, Leith, no more sunrises!'

He fell silent, but she was becoming accustomed to these long pauses. Was he remembering his other life, the life with Katherine? He would finish what he was saying—but only after he had weighed each of his words, and sorted his thoughts into order.

'No matter how terrible things get,' he said finally, his deep voice reaching into secret depths of her being, 'no matter how deeply we plunge into despair, there is always something, in every day, that brings us a special joy or pleasure.' His arms tightened momentarily as he gave her a quick hug. 'That's when we know for certain that we want a future.'

She felt tears prickling at her eyelids. Tears of tiredness or self-pity? she wondered. There was a soft patter of footsteps approaching, and she blinked furiously.

'Go to bed, Leith!' he added gruffly, turning her around and propelling her gently down the corridor before turning to greet the nurse who had come to sit with Anani.

CHAPTER FOUR

'HAVE you been to the place just south of here, with an unpronounceable name and a wealth of temples?'

Gabe's question startled her. They had worked for six days, rarely stopping for longer than it took to eat their meals.

Although she met him on the beach most mornings, and they walked back to the hospital together, personal subjects no longer arose. All their talk was of the patients — who they would see next, how others were recuperating, which people would need further operations.

'Mahabalipuram?'

'That's the one.'

Prakash was smiling at them. Idle conversation was rare in this theatre. Although Leith had always found it helped get through the day back home, here she found the quiet atmosphere peaceful and serene. It was a measure of her contentment with India that she could actually enjoy the silence of their tented workroom.

At times Gabe's deep voice would explain something to Prakash, or ask for some assistance, but its mellowness did not break the surface calm.

'No, I didn't get that far in my original sightseeing. Too much local colour to absorb.'

'That's good. We'll take two days off and go down there. Prakash tells me there's a great hotel, right on the beach. It will remind you of home.'

His blue eyes were sparkling mischievously at her over his mask.

Prakash explained, 'You will enjoy it, Sister. It is a wonderful place, very old. Greek traders came there two thousand years ago.'

'I think it's the almost infinite history of India that makes it so fascinating. Fancy being able to remember things that happened two thousand years ago, when our history—the European part of it—only goes back two hundred years.'

'There is plenty of history for you in southern India,' Prakash observed, pleased at her interest.

'I'm more interested in the lobster.' Gabe broke into their conversation.

'What lobster?' Leith asked.

Brown eyes twinkled at her. 'I told Gabe about the beautiful grilled lobster dish at the Mahabalipuram hotel.'

'Don't stop there, Prakash,' Gabe prompted. 'Tell her the name of the hotel.'

'It is Silversands Fun Resort. That is funny?' Prakash was puzzled by her quiet chuckle.

'No, Prakash,' she replied seriously, not wanting to hurt his feelings. 'It just seems an unlikely name for an Indian hotel. In Hawaii, or even on the Gold Coast in Australia, where Gabe and I live, it would fit right in, because tourists come to those places for the sun and sand and beaches.'

'But our beaches are good, are they not?'

'Your beaches are beautiful, unbelievable, Prakash! They are just. . .'

'Just?' queried Gabe, teasing her as she struggled to explain.

She shook her head reprovingly at him, and turned

her eyes again to the Indian. How could she explain the European cult of sun-worshipping that covered the beaches at home with thousands of people with practically no clothes on, all trying to make their white skins brown?

'We have a different beach culture,' she told him, quelling Gabe's quizzical glance with a censuring frown.

They drove south in the cool early hours of the morning, passing thatch-roofed villages, sheltered under tall palms and contrasting strongly with modern resort hotels that perched beside the glistening sea.

'Let's find the hotel, then come back to see the sights.' They followed a small sign and drove up to the 'resort', a simple seaside hotel, right on the beach.

'Temples first?'

Leith nodded. She was tired after the long week, and content to let Gabe make the decisions. Underlying the tiredness was a disquieting feeling that she knew was the result of her inexplicable attraction to the man with whom she was working so closely.

'Well, let's get going. Drop your bag in your room and we'll walk up to the village,' he suggested.

The carvings surpassed anything she had ever imagined, and she found it difficult to take in the magnitude of the work that long-ago tradesmen and artists had undertaken.

'They've carved the whole temple out of a single rock, and carved the elephant inside it.' The awe she felt was evident in her voice.

'Which came first—the elephant or the temple?' Gabe quipped.

He was a relaxed and undemanding companion.

Slowly they walked around the central site, taking in the elaborately carved rock face where humans, gods and animals vied for attention.

'It's too much to take in all at once.' She shook her head in wonder. 'I can't believe the diversity of the work, or the extent of it all.'

'Let's go back to the hotel. We can have lunch and a siesta, then come back later.'

'That's the best idea you've had since you suggested a couple of days off.' Leith sighed in relief, admitting to the tiredness that was threatening to overwhelm her.

A soft knocking came echoing into her dreams, but failed to wake her. She felt a cool touch on her shoulder, and turned to see Gabe bent over the bed.

'I did knock, but when you didn't answer I thought I'd better come in,' he told her, his voice a soothing murmur. 'If you don't wake up now you'll miss your dinner, and won't sleep tonight.'

Although he spoke softly his voice sent shivers of delight through her sleep-heavy body, which seemed to welcome his touch, as if hungry for a lover.

'What time is it?' She raised her eyes to his, unaware of the vulnerability in them that was a reflection of her blurred thoughts.

'Dinnertime! Or very nearly. We'll have time for a twilight drink by the beautiful beach before we savour the lobster. I'll wait for you under the third palm-tree from the left.'

She chuckled at his nonsense, taking in the blue, open-neck shirt that heightened the unusual colour of his eyes, and the grey tailored trousers that were smartly casual.

Her sense of smell, heightened by the exotic scents

of India, picked up the tang of a Guy Laroche aftershave fragrance that she had only savoured in testers on the counters of department stores. A *frisson* of excitement darted through her, and she felt her heart thumping erratically in her chest.

'I'll be there,' she promised and sprang off the bed, suddenly very aware of her crumpled jeans and shirt and unruly, slept-on hair.

Showering quickly, she pulled on filmy underwear, enjoying the sensual slither of satin on her sensitised skin, then reached for the pretty, strapless sun-frock of flowered silk that had been her one extravagance in the past twelve months.

Not that I've had much opportunity to wear it, she thought ruefully as she surveyed herself in the mirror. The splashy reds and yellows of the pattern, on a background of deep cream, flattered her golden colouring, warming her lightly tanned skin and contrasting with the golden streaks in her honey-brown hair. A touch of mascara darkened her thick lashes, and pale apricot lipstick added the final touch.

Quite a pretty girl, she told her reflection, unaware of the sparkle that excitement lent to her eyes or the enduring beauty of the fine bones that moulded her face. Turning her head, she lifted a hand to smooth her short hair against the nape of her neck, and let her fingers trail down the slender column of her throat.

Would he see her as a woman? she wondered.

Gabe rose from his chair on the grass beneath the palm-trees, and reached out to take her hand.

'You look lovely. I'm sorry that I've been working you so hard. You must have been exhausted to have slept like that. I should have made you have a day off earlier.'

'And would you have taken a day off as well?' She smiled cheekily at him as she asked the question.

'Probably not,' he admitted ruefully, 'and I wouldn't have achieved much without you, either. Polite conversation often leads us to say stupid things.'

'Don't I know it! Let's agree to refrain from polite conversation and only talk about the deep and meaningful.' A slight smile hovered on her lips as she teased him indulgently.

'I have a feeling that any "deep and meaningful" conversations with you would be simply your way of not telling me anything about yourself.'

'Maybe! One thing I will tell you, however, is that if I don't have a drink shortly I might die of thirst, and then there'll be no conversation! If you can attract the attention of the young lad who appears to be a waiter I will be thoroughly decadent and have a G and T, as the British colonists would have said.'

'I'm sorry. I'll order it for you, and try another Indian beer to see if I imagined how good the first one was.'

During dinner they discussed the temples they had seen, and made plans for more sightseeing in the morning. Leith described the great Parthasararthi Temple in Madras, with its brightly painted carvings depicting the many Indian gods.

The conversation drifted to Indian religions, led on to politics and then colonialism, touched on their work and veered off again on another tangent.

'That was the best meal I have ever had.' She pushed back her plate, empty save for the bare lobster shell.

'It's simple food, well cooked; that's the secret of a

really sensational taste treat,' Gabe expounded, mimicking the tones of a television gourmand, before adding sincerely, 'Those lobsters were probably caught this morning and brought directly to the hotel. It's the freshness that makes it so good.' He had obviously enjoyed his meal as much as she had.

'And the buttery sauce they served with them,' she sighed ecstatically. 'That's the type of thing that is probably so simple, yet drives an amateur mad trying to achieve the exact taste,' she added, responding to his undemanding presence.

'You like cooking?'

'Love it! I love cooking ordinary things like eggs on toast and very special things like grilled lobster with buttery sauce. India is driving me insane, with all the exotic spices and the fragrance of their foods. I'll be experimenting for years to come.'

She laughed at her own exuberance, which escaped so often now that she was relaxed and more at ease with Gabe Vincent.

'We work so closely, yet know so little about each other,' he murmured, reaching out to touch her cheek lightly, his fingers finding the scar on her temple, and probing at its contours.

Panic flared within her. His touch seared her, and she struggled to free herself from the tangling strands of intimacy his voice was weaving about them.

'Let's walk it off, shall we? That beach and moonlight and water combination is too good to waste.' She hoped he did not hear the shrillness in her voice, or recognise its cause.

Gabe put out a hand to help her out of her chair, and held hers in an affectionate clasp as he led the way across the grass towards the silvery sand. It was a companionable grasp—that of a friend, not a lover—but the intimacy of it was too much for Leith and she pulled away, pausing to slip off her sandals to cover her rejection of his touch.

They strolled in silence, the night entwining them in its magic, the sand soft and still warm beneath their feet.

'I haven't walked on a beach with a woman since my wife died.'

He broke the silence so abruptly that Leith gasped as she drew in a quick breath of amazement. Unable to think of any reply to such a statement, she said the first thing that came into her head.

'I knew Katherine from school. She was several years ahead of me, but so kind and so beautiful. We all loved her.'

'Everyone who saw her loved her.' The words were wrenched from him, as if the physical effort of saying them was almost too much to bear. He paced away from her and then back, as if unable to speak without moving his body from one place to another, while his talented fingers twisted round each other, whitening with the effort of his words.

'So many people loved her that the fact that she chose me seemed like a miracle. Too big a miracle, too miraculous an occurrence, for me to ever question it. That's what made it so hard afterwards.'

'After she died?' She spoke with quiet sympathy, moved by the emotion that this man was struggling to contain. She willed him to continue, acknowledging the easing of pain she had felt after her confession to Ian Musgrave, what seemed like light-years ago.

'After we found out about the cancer.' His voice was hoarse, as if twisted by the remembered anguish, and

Leith felt tears prickling in her eyes and her throat tightening with the compassion she felt for this man.

The straining voice continued, 'After she became ill and begged me to agree to a totally unnecessary operation. After. . .after I said yes.' He had paused in his pacing, and his voice had dropped to an almost inaudible mutter. She reached out to take his writhing hands in hers, to give him human contact while he wrestled with ghosts that had to be exorcised.

'Is that why she married me all along? Because of what I did? What I knew? Did she think that I could keep her beauty? Was that why I was chosen?' he asked harshly, the words loud and explosive in that idyllic setting, his hands gripping hers with a ferocity that made her wince.

She could not understand the questions, let alone provide answers. What monstrous self-doubt was lurking behind the surface calm of Gabe Vincent? She could not imagine, could not hazard a guess!

So on that moonlit beach, with the magic of the night sky soft above them, she stood quietly, her fingers kneading his, as she swallowed the tears that threatened to flow.

She felt the plummeting depths of his pain and torment, and all her instincts prompted her to reach out, to take him in her arms, to hold and soothe him.

Or was that just an excuse?

An inner demon asked the question. She could not deny the chemistry of her body, could not deny that his potent attraction sent her pulses racing and the blood flowing hotly to the most sensitive parts of her being. Even now, as she sought to comfort him, traitorous tremors within her reflected the power of his sensual appeal.

Rejecting the impulse to hold him close, to offer the comfort of her body, she dropped his hands and turned to face the restless sea.

'Race you to the water's edge!' she challenged. The words trembled on her lips as she forced herself to bring the situation back under control.

'Five yards' start and I'll still beat you!'

She fled, running as if for her life, running from the danger that this man represented. Beaches and moonlight and shimmering seas were for lovers, not for two maimed people, each seeking their own salvation from the pain of the past.

Like two kids set free from school, they frolicked in the shallow wash of the waves, kicking sprays of water into the air, where they shone with the milky opalescence of pearls flung upwards by a mad juggler.

'I hope you realise, Sister Robinson, that I have probably ruined a good pair of trousers with all of this idiotish behaviour.'

'Idiotish. What a lovely word.' She echoed it reflectively. 'It's a long time since I've been idiotish. Give them to me when we go back, and I'll get Colin to take care of them.'

'Colin?'

'He's the gardener-cum-laundry-man at the nunnery. I'll grant you it's an unusual name for an Indian, but his family were old retainers to British merchants, and he was named after one of their ancestors.'

'Are you telling me that an old gardener does all the laundry for the hospital?'

She laughed at his astonishment. 'No, no! The hospital laundry—sheets and such—goes into town. Colin looks after the nursing staff, and there's no one who can make my uniforms look better!'

HEALING LOVE

'It's the person inside the uniform that makes them so attractive.' His voice dropped to a deep whisper, startling her with its intensity.

She spun around to find herself scant inches from his chest, the faint impression of his aftershave hovering in the air between them, seeming to cling to his unlikely remark.

'You're a constant source of pleasure, you know.' His hands reached out to hold her shoulders and she raised her eyes to question his, while soft waves washed around their feet.

'I look across the table and see concern and concentration in your pretty eyes,' he said, his voice a murmuring echo of the restless sea. 'Then the graft sits right, the stitches finish neatly. I catch a glimpse of pride and approval from you, and feel the satisfaction in my job that I lost years ago.'

'Any nurse must admire your work. I'm not an exception.' She hoped her cool response hid the thundering heartbeats his closeness had precipitated.

'Oh, yes, you are, Sister Robinson — an exception in many ways. You do not flirt or chatter or ask for praise. You are calm, cool, competent and so self-possessed that you intrigue me.' His head moved as if his eyes were scrutinising her, but shadows hid his face and she could not guess at his expression.

'Can't you simply accept that what you see is what you get? I'm just a very ordinary person who loves her job and admires professionalism when she sees it.'

She held his gaze steadily, resolutely quelling the flickers of fire that his touch was sending through her veins.

'Would such an ordinary person object if another ordinary person leaned forward like this——' his mouth hovered above hers, lips pale in the moonlight '—then kissed her like this?'

It was a gentle, exploratory kiss, like that of two teenagers on a first date. No passion, no commitment— just a sweet, tentative tasting of each other's lips, engendering a sweet, flaring excitement that signalled the possibility of something more in the future.

Yet Leith felt her blood fizzing in her veins, sending prickles of desire teasing at her nipples.

'Shall we walk again?'

His voice broke the spell. Despite the warmth of the night, she felt a coldness as he lifted his head, leaving her lips bereft, her body hungering for his touch.

He took her hand, and this time she did not seek to pull away. It felt right and comfortable in Gabe's larger one; it was a continued contact! Together they savoured the magic of the moonlight, marvelling at the luminous path that stretched across the shining water, and drinking in the intoxicating fragrances that were part of the magic of India.

'Do you want a drink before you go to bed?' His voice, asking such a mundane question, thrilled her, and she felt herself blushing as she shook her head.

'I know I shouldn't be tired after sleeping all afternoon, but I can hardly keep my eyes open.'

'I'll walk you to your room.'

They made their way across the wide marble-tiled foyer, threading through the elegant cane chairs that were scattered about, and slowly climbed the staircase to the first floor.

Tired as she was, Leith felt a reluctance to let him go, and her hand clung to his until he stopped outside her door and turned her tenderly towards him, bending his head to kiss her once more.

Was it typical of a second kiss? Afterwards she could not remember.

She knew that her lips reached up hungrily to his, and that, as the pressure of his mouth grew more demanding, she welcomed his tongue, teasing at it with her own, as they tasted each other's special magic.

Their bodies moved closer, drawn by a need to know shapes and textures. His hands sought the contours of her back, searching restlessly over her satiny skin, while hers crept around his shoulders to feel the prickling coarseness of his hair, and the strong bones of his neck.

The intensity deepened suddenly, beyond the bounds of a simple goodnight embrace, and her breathing quickened. She felt his chest heaving against her as if he gasped for air. Bound by a timeless magic, they lingered thus, for dizzying minutes of enchantment, until they drew apart, breathing deeply, and he opened the door and eased her reluctantly through it.

'Sleep as long as you can,' he whispered against her hair, 'and I'll see you downstairs when you're ready for the day.'

She felt his lips brush across her cheek, and her fingers trailed from his unwillingly as he disappeared down the passageway.

This is a friendship, she told herself firmly, breathing deeply in an effort to still her racing pulse. A very pleasant, relaxed, companionable interlude in both our lives that will make the memories of India so much sweeter. She smiled at her reflection in the mirror, winking at the sparkling eyes and rosy cheeks that belied her cautious words, then she slipped out of her clothes and into bed, more at ease with herself than she had been for a long time.

* * *

'I thought you'd be sleeping in.'

His voice startled her as she walked on the beach in the pale dawn light.

'I'm in the habit of early morning walks now. My day wouldn't be right if I haven't seen the sun rise out of the water.'

This beach was quieter. A few fishermen pushed their beautiful, high-prowed boats out into the waves, but by comparison with Madras it was deserted.

'Mmm, feel the warmth of that sun. Maybe we should have an early breakfast and finish our sightseeing before it gets too hot.'

Leith tried to analyse her feelings. He had met her this morning as a friend, which was what she hoped they were. Yet she felt a disappointment, a vague longing for some sign that she was just a little bit special—that the evening they had spent together had some meaning for him as well.

You should be glad he's reacting this way, she told herself with acerbity. What can you offer a man like him?

'I'll give you those trousers for your Colin,' he continued in matter-of-fact tones, and she shrugged her idle fantasies away.

'Men,' she muttered in disgust, 'thinking of practicalities on a tropical beach at sunrise. Come on, I'll race you back to breakfast—last one has to pay.'

She flung the last words over her shoulder as she raced towards the lawns that spread down from the hotel to the beach. Her slim brown legs flashed under her filmy cotton skirt, and her laughter echoed over the silver sands and glinting water.

'There's a competitive streak in you, with all these "race you" challenges you throw out.' Gabe was panting slightly as he collapsed into his chair, and there was a sparkle of fine, pale sand among the wiry dark hairs on his tanned forearms.

Leith resisted the temptation to reach over and brush it away, and merely laughed at him.

'Comes of growing up with three brothers. If you couldn't compete, you missed out.'

'Where was that, and what do these wonder boys do now?'

'Western Australia, and they are all on properties—sheep and wheat. Tim, the youngest, is still unmarried and helps Dad at home, but the older two have places of their own.'

'And you are duly proud of them.'

'Of course I am. They're the best family a girl could have.'

'Yet you washed ashore at the Gold Coast. That's a long way from the people you obviously love.'

He sounded genuinely interested, but she could hardly blurt out the words that sprang to mind—But close to the man I believed would be mine for life.

'I travelled around Australia when I finished my general degree, and did my surgical training back at Gold Coast. After that I seemed to stick. Do you have brothers and sisters?'

'I do,' he told her gravely. 'Sometimes it seems like dozens of them, although there are only five. I'm the youngest, and my three sisters and both my brothers are married. I find that rarely a week goes by without one or other of them landing on my doorstep.'

Leith wondered how the cool, correct Katherine that she remembered had coped with an exuberant extended Italian family.

'It's the sort of mob that buys eight-seater vans as

their family car,' he continued. 'At last count I think I had seventeen nieces and nephews, but the numbers change almost daily. The general impression of the Vincents *en masse* is kids and movement and laughter.'

His voice dropped to a murmur, so the portrait of this riotous family that he was attempting to paint with his words became blurred.

She saw a shadow flicker across his face. Had he longed for children? Was the sadness for all the ones he and Katherine would never have? She longed to reach out a hand and touch his arm in solace, but the mood of the morning forbade such intimacies.

A hollow-bellied dog ran across the lawn to the beach, and three small brown children in hot pursuit diverted them both. Leith's eyes softened as she watched them, and the overpowering urge to hold a child's chubby body and smell the baby softness came over her with a rush.

One day, she promised herself, a slight smile on her lips as she saw them disappear among the fringing palms; one day soon. The money she was earning here was bringing the dream that much closer.

CHAPTER FIVE

'How many on the list for today, Leith?' They had been back at work for four days, and the heavy workload was beginning to tell.

'I've listed four category one patients, a second graft for Anani, plus another excision and bit of fancy work for the young man you did that first day.'

'Good girl. I don't think I could have coped with another day like yesterday.'

They were walking slowly up from what Leith considered 'her' beach, having met as she was turning for home. Her heart had leapt, as always, at the sight of his figure approaching along the sands. She tried to ignore this physical response to his presence and concentrate her mind on the work they had to achieve together.

An easy alliance bound them, forged in their shared efforts in the small theatre and strengthened by the pleasurable weekend they had shared at Mahabalipuram.

'Do you have to push yourself so hard? Is there some reason why you want to get it all finished in two months?'

It was a question she would not have asked a week ago. She felt he was driven by something, and she no longer supposed it was concern over the interruption to his career.

'Still having ethical or moral doubts about taking the

money?' One black eyebrow quirked interrogatively, and her heart skipped another beat.

'More like doubts about your ability to survive if you keep going at this rate,' she countered. 'I've heard about your midnight visits to the patients you're concerned about. It's too much for one man to be doing, Gabe.'

'Look who's talking,' he teased. 'Kala tells me that you've been scrubbing out the steriliser after dinner every second night, because the other staff are too busy.'

'I like to know it's done properly,' she answered defensively. 'If I do it myself I can have an easy night's sleep.'

'What's left of the night, after you've finished that job. I'm quite certain that that antiquated bit of machinery did not come in the packaged theatre. Some hospital has our state-of-the-art steriliser and we have their old model.'

'I didn't know you specialists knew what a steriliser looked like. I thought you all believed that instruments arrived in sterile packages.'

She grinned at him as she spoke.

'Like our gowns and masks back home.' Gabe sighed. 'It all seems so far away.'

'Are you missing it?'

Leith heard the surprise in her voice, and knew that it was because she rarely thought of home, content to enjoy the variety and excitement of whatever this unfamiliar land might offer her.

'Not really. Sometimes I hate to even think of going back.'

He sighed again as he continued, 'There's so much that I want to do, Leith, so many things I want to achieve that I know I must go back. It's hard to do anything without money, and I can earn more—and earn it more easily—at home.'

She found this materialistic side of Gabe at odds with everything else that she knew about him, but then he had similar doubts about her.

'If we don't get moving a little faster we won't earn much today,' she said tartly.

They hurried up off the beach, and Leith held his arm to steady herself while she slipped off her sandals and shook out the sand. The warmth of the contact shook her slightly, although she performed this little ritual each morning.

'To get back to your original question, no, we don't have to push ourselves so hard.' He placed a slight emphasis on the plurals. 'But there's another little job looming on the horizon, and I'll feel happier about accepting it if we are well ahead of schedule here.'

'There's another job that you'd take before you finished here? Would you leave these people to some other surgeon after winning their trust the way you have?'

Disbelief and disgust made her voice shrill.

'Calm down. I wouldn't ever leave a job half finished, although I may take a break for a few days, if I can see a good opportunity to pause in our work.'

He kept walking as he was speaking, and she found herself hurrying close by his side to catch what he was saying.

'Remember Prakash and me discussing an extra pair of hands?'

'Yes!' She was surprised that the subject hadn't come up again, now that she considered it.

'Well, I've found them. The cavalry is about to arrive and relieve our besieged fort!'

'What are you talking about?' She was taking two steps to each one of his and was becoming breathless, as the excitement of his ideas had quickened his stride.

'Just that I, Gabe Vincent, happen to run the cosmetic surgery speciality programme back home, and people wishing to study on the programme are usually only too willing to fall in with my suggestions,' he explained in a voice of mock-superiority.

'Don't I know it,' Leith replied with feeling. 'I've seen the poor young doctors falling over themselves to beat others to the door, just for the honour of holding it open for you.'

'And to think I thought you'd never noticed me,' Gabe murmured provocatively.

'Well, I certainly wouldn't have opened the door!' She felt aggrieved, although she couldn't explain the feeling. 'What's all this leading up to anyway?'

'Just that one of these hopeful students will be arriving here the day after tomorrow. He's done his primaries, so should be able to help Prakash and generally keep an eye on the post-op people. And that means. . .'

This time his habit of pausing irritated her as some faint memory awoken by his words niggled at the back of her mind.

'What?' she asked ungraciously, urging him to finish.

'Just this!' He paused in mid-step and grinned wickedly down at her before continuing, 'When we finish all the first grafts, and while we wait for them to settle down enough for further work, I would like, with your permission, Sister, to slip away to Abu Dhabi for a few days.'

His silken smooth tone might mock, but his eyes laughed down at her, inviting her to share the fun. The remote man she had first met was mellowing. Was the Archangel Gabriel coming down from his clouds?

'Abu where?' she asked vaguely, distracted by her errant thoughts.

'Dhabi, in the United Arab Emirates—not that far from here as the private plane flies. Will you fly with me to the casbah?'

'What are you talking about, Gabe Vincent?'

'I am talking, my dear, about a little job that awaits the two of us, worth more humble money than our greedy little hearts ever dreamed of. A member of an aristocratic family has a son who suffered facial injuries in a shooting accident. He was out in the desert when it happened, and some of the shotgun pellets lodged in his face, and the wounds became infected. We are to patch him up, to the best of our poor ability.'

'"We"? Which "we"?' she demanded.

'Why, you and me, we, that's which we. The patients here will be able to spare us for a few days—eventually. Say you'll come, Leith, please do. It will be another country for you to visit and a great adventure for us to share.'

'A great adventure for us to share.' The words echoed in her head, evoking a warmth and excitement that lightened her step and coloured her cheeks.

She missed Gabe on the beach, some of the savour going out of her morning ritual. Officially she had the day off, as the theatre was being thoroughly cleaned, and the two doctors had planned to run a clinic for the post-op patients who were to be discharged from hospital that day.

She sauntered along, spraying the sand ahead of her feet as she kicked into it. Why was there so little appeal in having a whole day off? There were many places she hadn't visited right here in Madras, so she could do some leisurely sightseeing, write some overdue letters to family and friends back home, or even catch up on some sleep.

'Bother!' she muttered aloud as a particularly vicious kick sent the sand over her clothes and into her hair.

What were the words Gabe had used? That there was always one small thing in every day that made it worth living? That wasn't quite right, she decided, but it was more or less what he meant. Enough of this dejection, Leith. Get on with the day, and let the moment come to you!

Having chided herself for her pessimism, she moved more briskly, the gloom she had felt lifting suddenly as she watched some children clambering over the slick body of an ox as they washed him in the shallow water.

'Oh, Leith, I was afraid you might have gone with Gabe!'

Kala greeted her with anxious relief when she finally arrived back at the temporary hospital.

'What's up, Kala, and where's Gabe gone?'

'He's collecting the new doctor from the airport, and the plane must be late. Prakash has started the clinic, but needs someone to speak to the people after he has seen them. They need to know about home care, because we cannot keep them all here.'

'It's standard post-operative stuff, Kala. Sister Ramend could handle it if you are busy.'

'That is the trouble, Leith. She is sick, and I am in charge of the beds today, so. . .'

'So would I take over?'

'I know it is your day off, and you work very hard.'

Concern was apparent in Kala's soft eyes, but there was also a pleading insistence that Leith could not deny.

'I was wondering how to fill in my day,' she said lightly, smiling at the woman who had become a friend as well as associate. 'I just hope I don't confuse them. I'm more used to doing this for eye patients!'

'The most important thing to remember,' Leith said slowly, allowing the young nurse who was translating for those who did not understand English to repeat her words, 'is that it takes time. Because of the scar tissue from the graft, you might think you look worse than you did before——'

'Would that be possible?'

A young man who had lost an eye in the holocaust interjected, and Leith grinned at him.

He had used her as the straight man for his comic remarks throughout her talk, and she appreciated the humour that had lightened the morning's session.

'But in time it will settle down. Your new skin may feel stiff, and as it heals it will be itchy, scaly and red, but if you are careful, and take care of it as I have told you, by this time next year people will be admiring your wonderful complexions.'

Will they? she added silently to herself, looking at the swathed faces turned so eagerly towards her.

'You must all come back to see the doctors next week, but if you notice any changes——'

'Redness, soreness, moisture,' they chanted in a chorus, and she smiled at their enthusiasm.

'Yes. Any of that, come back immediately.'

There was the sound of applause from the back of the room—one person clapping?

She peered towards the noise, but the patients were all on their feet, moving towards their friends or shuffling towards the door. She sat down at the desk to make some notes on the margins of the pages she had hastily prepared for the talk, so it was not until a shadow fell across her that she identified the source of the ironic accolade.

'Hello, darling. Pleased to see me?'

'Mark!'

Her heart beat a frantic tattoo against her ribcage, and her stomach churned so wildly that she thought she would be sick. She gripped the edge of the desk, willing the panic to subside.

'What are you doing here?' The words came out as a croak, twisted by the tension that was paralysing her.

'Didn't you know I was coming?'

'No!'

The word came out with explosive force. How could she have known? Should she have guessed? She recalled Gabe's conversation about hopeful students, recalled that it had rung a vague bell in her mind at the time. . .but Mark?

She realised now that she hadn't thought of him since arriving in India—apart from that brief moment in Anani's room. Surely that meant she was cured? But if that was so, why was she sitting here, so sick and trembly?

He had moved away from the desk and was walking around the room, which had originally been a small chapel. He opened and closed the doors that led out on to the deep veranda, then prowled around, touching things here and there, like a cat making itself familiar with a new home.

'Then it's shock that's sent you into this catatonic state. May I prescribe something for it? Let's see — apply warmth for shock, don't we, Sister?'

He moved towards her, but she raised her hands in a mute protest.

'Just stay away from me, Mark,' she said shakily.

'What? No delighted welcome for the long-lost lover? We were good together, Leith,' he murmured.

He came close, and leant over the desk, so that she could feel his breath moving against her bowed cheek.

'Have you forgotten, darling?'

She felt his hand touch her hair, and pushed herself back into the chair, looking up into his laughing brown eyes. He was a handsome devil, she realised irrationally, tanned and blond — the very image of the sun-bronzed Aussie.

'It could still be good.' He almost purred the words. 'Nothing heavy, my sweet, no strings or promises — just a giving and taking of pleasure to while away the lonely nights so far from home.'

She summoned up a hollow laugh, and rose to her feet, backing slightly away from the desk, but taking care to keep it between herself and this unwelcome intruder.

'You obviously haven't spent a day in Theatre with Gabe Vincent. Wait till tomorrow night and see if you feel like anything but sleep to while away the nights,' she told him crisply, hiding her dismay under her professional façade. 'Thanks, but no, thanks, Mark. I'm here to work, and, in between, I sleep.'

'But Leith, surely you can show me the sights, or have dinner with me occasionally — for old times' sake.'

'I don't think so, Mark. Most of my memories of the "old times" are still fairly painful.'

She gathered up her notes and fled, leaving him standing alone in the bare room.

Her reaction to Mark had shocked her, not because of its turbulence but because, after the initial lurch of surprise, what she had felt had been fear! Her mind sought an answer. Why fear?

'Is there a fire?'

She had rushed out of the door and cannoned into Gabe, who held her steady, looking down at her with laughing eyes.

When he looks at me like that I feel as if I'm melting. The wayward notion penetrated the chaos in her mind, and she unerringly identified the reason for her fear.

'I must go,' she mumbled incoherently, taking off down the corridor as if the hounds of hell were at her heels.

'There's some bleeding beneath the graft, Sister!'

Gabe's voice was sharp, and Leith looked questioningly at him over her mask, but his eyes were on the job, and the little she could see of his face gave nothing away.

She reached for a cotton applicator stick and leaned forward to ease it in under the translucent skin, removing the tiny clot before Gabe completed his stapling. She had seen Prakash do it many times, but he was not in Theatre this morning. Mark was gowned and gloved, but had only observed so far.

She twisted the thin stick in her fingers, and removed the offending clot, but her fingers were shaking with a new tension that was making the atmosphere both heavy and tiring.

As each stage of an operation proceeded, Gabe explained what he was doing and why. He spoke with a precision that matched his skill, imparting the necessary information clearly and concisely.

Knowing most of what he was saying, Leith had tuned out, and her mind was drifting through realms of its own while her body performed the allotted tasks with an automatic expertise.

The day had passed more swiftly than usual, she thought as she watched the last patient wheeled from the room, and turned to push the drip stand aside so she could move her trolley.

'Are you with us, Sister Robinson?'

She glanced up at Gabe, to see an angry glare in his blue eyes and a frown marring the skin beneath his cap.

'I'm sorry, I thought you were talking to Dr Armstrong.'

'I was talking *of* Dr Armstrong. It seems he would like to have dinner with you this evening.'

Dropping the dressings she was about to count on to the stainless steel surface, Leith looked from one to the other. Gabe was stripping off his gloves, although his eyes were fixed on her with a blankness that she found quite chilling. Mark looked ready to beat a strategic retreat.

'He asked *you* if he could take *me* out to dinner?' she demanded, incensed by Mark's duplicity and by Gabe's consideration of the idea. 'What does it have to do with you?'

'I'm the head of the team,' Gabe explained stiffly. 'I suppose he considered it a politeness.'

Leith drew a deep breath. The day had begun badly when Gabe had missed their morning walk on the beach—again—and Mark's presence had made her nervous and edgy. Now this. . .! All the pent-up emotions were about to escape, and she no longer cared!

'Oh, really?' Sarcasm dripped from the words. 'Do all doctors assume that if there's only one nurse about she naturally "belongs" to the "head of the team"? Did he think you might be tired of me, or be willing to share?' She turned furiously towards Mark as she asked the question, before swinging back to glare at the senior man.

'Are you, Gabe? Would you, Dr Vincent?'

'You're being ridiculous, Leith!' That was Mark. She frowned contemptuously at him, and he drifted noiselessly out of the suddenly cramped theatre.

'Am I?' she shouted at his departing back.

'Yes, you're making too much of it. It was a politeness, that's all!' Gabe said quickly as he tried to placate her, but she rejected his soothing words.

'If you really believe that, then you're not as smart as I thought you were. It's typical of the whole doctor-nurse scenario. You might not believe this, but I work just as hard as you do.'

She scowled at him over her mask as her shaking fingers attempted to remove it.

'I have great skills that took as many years of study to achieve as yours did, yet you doctors continue to treat all nurses as lackeys—second-class citizens, as belongings that come with the job. You graduate and are presented with a white coat, stethoscope and nurse——'

'That's ridiculous——'

'Is it?'

The strings came undone, and she turned away,

pulling off the suffocating mask and dropping it into the bin. As she stood there she felt the sudden rage draining out of her, leaving a cold and curiously empty shell.

'And what was your reply?' she asked quietly.

'My reply to what?'

His voice was icily remote, but she had to ask!

'To the dinner invitation, of course.'

'Leith——'

He had agreed! She knew it. He had told Mark to go ahead and ask her out!

'It doesn't matter,' she said abruptly, and left the room, a bitter disappointment welling inside her.

She avoided them both over the next week, taking her meals into Anani's room, where she listened to tales of life in India and shared memories of home with the wide-eyed girl. In the mornings she walked through the streets around the temporary hospital, marvelling at the architecture of the old buildings that owed so much to the days of the British raj, yet had a uniqueness that was pure Indian.

She found small temples in out-of-the-way places, bright with offerings of fresh flowers, fruit or grain, and the mystical quality of the country soothed her turbulent spirit and calmed her perturbed mind. Unconsciously she absorbed more than just the sights and sounds and scent of this exotic place; she found the thing that was at the heart of every Indian—an acceptance of 'karma'.

She would wait! If there was to be something special in her life—she dared not tempt it too far by labelling the 'something'—then it would happen!

* * *

'I'd like a word with you when we finish here, Sister.'

Leith looked up at Gabe, but he rarely met her eyes these days. Prakash had resumed his place in Theatre, and silence reigned. Mark had taken over the wards, attending to the growing number of post-operative patients and helping with the regular outpatients clinics.

'Leave the theatre for Kala to scrub, and have a cup of coffee with me.' He spoke abruptly, then turned and left the room, obviously expecting her to follow meekly in his wake.

Which I will dutifully do, she told herself with a grin as she walked behind his broad back down the corridor towards the small cell he used as an office.

'I've made arrangements to go to Abu Dhabi on Friday,' he said as he pulled out a chair for her. One of the wardsmen arrived with a pot of coffee, and Leith waited as he poured them each a mug of the lethal brew.

'Do you think they might have real coffee in Abu Dhabi?' Leith grimaced as she took her first sip, and watched the wariness in Gabe's eyes fade as he replied to her light remark.

'It'll probably be Turkish, and thick enough to hold the spoon upright.'

He grinned at her, and her insides melted.

So much for karma, she told herself ruefully, but smiled back at him, relieved to feel the tension between them slipping away so easily.

'What are the plans?'

She thrust aside any ethical doubts she might have had about this excursion. It would be, as Gabe had said, an adventure!

'We'll leave here in the morning. The representative

from Abu Dhabi has made all the arrangements. It seems that many Indians have migrated to the Emirates and opened small businesses there, so even in Madras there is a person to act as Consul for them. He has taken care of the exit and re-entry requirements here.'

'What, no Passport Control, or Customs or forms to complete in triplicate?' Leith asked.

'Just shows how money can smooth the path of the traveller. A car will collect us at ten o'clock to convey us——'

'In style, I hope.'

'Of course.' Gabe bowed his head towards her, before finishing, 'In style, to the airport where the private jet will await our pleasure.'

'Maybe not quite! I bet they wouldn't fly us home, even if we asked nicely.'

'I suppose not, but we can pretend.' He smiled at her for a moment, then asked more seriously, 'Do you want to go home?'

Leith was so startled by his question that she nearly dropped her mug.

'Of course not!' she protested vehemently. 'Well, not yet anyway. Not until our job is finished.'

She looked across the desk at Gabe, who was frowning at the pen that twirled between his fingers.

'What makes you ask?'

'I haven't seen much of you lately... I've missed you on the beach...'

'I've been exploring,' she explained hurriedly, alarmed by the hope that surged through her at his hesitant admission. 'Checking out the neighbourhood.'

'Avoiding me?'

What could she say?

'I thought you and Mark would be driving over each day.'

'Did you know Mark before he came here?'

The question surprised her, and the quiet voice in which he asked it puzzled her even more.

'Yes,' she answered baldly, not willing to pursue the subject, but unable to lie.

She faced the fear she had felt at Mark's arrival. It had been fear that Mark would betray their past relationship—and its consequences!

'I wondered.'

Silence deepened between them—not the comfortable silence that she usually enjoyed with Gabe, but a strained tension that was destroying her hard-won peace of mind. She forced herself to think of work.

'What equipment should we take with us?'

That startled him, she thought, as his fingers stilled on the pen and he looked sharply across at her.

'I've made a list. It's only the specialist things that they might not have. Most of the hospitals in these Arab states are exceptionally well-equipped.'

'If you let me have it I'll pack what you need.'

'Is that part of your special training or mine?' He asked the question ruefully, and Leith felt a flood of colour rising to her cheeks.

'I don't mind doing anything to help,' she told him forcefully. 'It's just being treated like a belonging that really makes me angry.'

'Oh, I did gather that,' Gabe murmured.

His eyes sparkled mischievously, and some of the lines of strain and tiredness seemed to ease in his face as he grinned at her. He put down the pen and reached a lean hand across the desk.

'Peace?'

'Peace.'

She reached out to grasp his fingers as she echoed his word. Their hands intertwined, as if seeking, of their own volition, some closer bond. She felt a quickening in the rhythm of her heart and a brief flaring spark of delight.

'There's a patient I'd like you to. . .'

Mark's head appeared at the open door, but the words dried up when he realised that Gabe was not alone.

Snatching her hand away from Gabe's, Leith rose to her feet and moved towards the door.

'I'll get that list later,' she said breathlessly, aware that her embarrassment must be obvious as heat burnt in her cheeks.

'Ten o'clock, Friday, Leith!'

As Gabe's confirming words followed her out of the door she heard them as a promise, an affirmation of something special that would be theirs to share — even if it was only an adventure.

'What's happening on Friday?'

Mark must have been waiting for her to leave Anani's room much later that night. He fell into step beside her as she walked back down the corridor towards her own retreat.

'I'm going to Abu Dhabi.'

'Gabe mentioned something about a little job he'd picked up over there.'

He reached out to open her door for her, before adding musingly, 'He certainly knows where the money is.'

Although he echoed her own thoughts, she was

irritated by Mark's words, and by his familiarity as he followed her into the tiny bedroom.

'I didn't know you were going with him. Do I detect something more than a purely professional relationship?'

'Of course not, Mark. He needs a nurse who knows his methods, that's all.'

She reached into the small cupboard as she was talking, pulling out her bathrobe and toiletry bag and hoping her unwelcome guest would get the message.

'We've been working darned hard here for the last month, and it'll be a bit of a break as well. In case you haven't noticed, regular days off are not part of the schedule.'

'Haven't noticed?' He flopped down on to her bed. 'I can't tell you how much I'm looking forward to this weekend. With the cat away, this mouse will play!'

He winked at her, his teasing smile lighting up his face, tempting her to join him in the joke.

'I had hoped that you'd be around to play with me,' he added seductively, and Leith cringed as she remembered the times she had responded so joyfully to these or similar words.

'Not this weekend,' she answered lightly. 'Now get going. I've got to get showered and changed before my date comes to take me out to dinner.'

'You are seeing him socially.' Mark hurled the accusation at her, an angry venom in the words.

'Don't jump to conclusions, Mark,' she responded wearily. 'I'm having dinner with Anani's parents. Her brother is collecting me after his visit to her, and I said I'd be ready by seven.'

She glanced at her watch, hesitated, then decided to say what was really bothering her.

'And even if I were seeing him, what business is it of yours? Our relationship was over a long time ago, Mark.'

'Was it really, Leith? Can you deny that there's still something between us? I can't.'

He grabbed her by the hand as she moved to leave the room, and, sitting up on the bed, he pulled her towards him.

'I see you each day, so beautiful! These last twelve months have matured you somehow, or maybe I had begun to take you for granted.'

His hand reached up to ruffle her short hair, and his fingers trailed down her cheeks, leaving a path of coldness.

'You tantalise me, Leith. I see those big brown eyes glance at me across the room, or smell your perfume — Miss Dior still, isn't it? — as you pass me in the corridor. I can't help remembering, darling. . .'

With a gentle pressure he tried to ease her towards him, but she stood immobile in his grasp, still as a statue, and as unmoved. He had a polished seduction routine. She had seen him at it so often, and remembered the searing jealousy that she had always felt when he went into action.

'Just practising,' he would joke if she objected to his flirting. 'Keeping my hand in in case you ever leave me!'

She pulled away from him, rejecting the memories at the same time as she rejected the man.

'Nor can I,' she said candidly, 'but I remember Caroline, and all the words that would have been better left unspoken. It's over, Mark, and has been for so long that all the embers are dead and the ashes scattered on the wind. Now get out of here, so I can get ready for my night out. Some of us still have a social life.'

She pushed him out of the door.

The air-conditioned limousine whisked them through the chaotic traffic and out to the airport with an effortless ease. There they entered through a side-gate and drove to the gangway of a sleek jet that, to Leith's inexperienced eyes, looked almost as large as a jumbo.

'I'm Nate Wilcox, and I'll be your pilot.'

The bright young American welcomed them with a friendly handshake and introduced them to Nina, his lovely blonde wife, who would be acting as their hostess on the trip.

The interior of the plane resembled the opulent drawing-rooms of the rich and famous that Leith had seen illustrated in fashion magazines. In a bemused trance she sank into the deep softness of an armchair, rubbing her fingers through the deep furrows in the rich velveteen covering.

'Champagne and caviare, madam?' Gabe queried, smiling at the wonder in her face.

'We'll have the champagne after take-off, and there is caviare if you'd like it,' Nina assured him, and Leith looked at her in amazement.

'He's just joking,' she protested. 'We don't need champagne, and I've never even tasted caviare!'

'You speak for yourself, Sister Robinson,' said Gabe, reclining in his chair in a lordly manner. 'I'm off duty for the next six hours, and I'm looking forward to my champagne. I'll even sample the caviare — see if it's as good as the other I've tasted!'

He waved a languid hand at Nina as he spoke, and both girls laughed. It was good to see Gabe relax like this, Leith thought, feeling her own tensions slipping away as she slipped into his holiday mood.

As the plane slid effortlessly into the sky Leith turned to the large porthole nearest her chair, and watched Madras grow smaller until it disappeared behind them.

'Champagne?'

Nina's voice drew her attention away from the window.

'Thank you!' She smiled as she took a flute from the tray and lifted it in salute towards Gabe. As she sipped the cool liquid, enjoying the sensation as the tiny bubbles exploded against her tongue, she felt her body relax, and knew that she would sleep through this, her second international plane trip, just as she had through the first. Would that sleep be as troubled?

CHAPTER SIX

LEITH woke with a feeling of wonder. The soft contours of the armchair provided a haven, and she had slept soundly. The ornate room hummed through the sky, and, peering through the window, she saw water below her, with small specks of ships scattered on its blueness.

Across from her, Gabe lay back in his chair, his lean, well-muscled body relaxed and at ease, his eyes closed in sleep. Long black lashes lay still on his tanned cheeks, softening the bony contours of his face. She wondered if the strain of the merciless work schedule he imposed on himself had begun to tell. Were the lines across his brow deeper?

After weeks of studying him surreptitiously, she enjoyed the freedom his unconscious state gave her, and her eyes sought to imprint each tiny detail in her mind. His black hair was tousled and a stray lock flopped on his forehead. Her eyes lingered on his pale lips, then traced along his jaw as a shiver spread through her.

His neck rose like a strong column from the open neck of his cotton shirt, and her loving gaze followed the corded tendon down towards his shoulder, while her fingers longed to trace its path.

One arm was flung over the arm of the chair, and she noticed again the muscular strength of his limbs that contrasted so strangely with the delicate, tapering beauty of his hands. She squirmed in her seat, unexpectedly restless at the sight of those hands—or at the thoughts that they evoked.

A great longing filled her as she imagined their touch, lingering on her body, inflaming it to fever pitch as they explored her soft contours and secret places.

Colour stained her cheeks as Gabe stirred and his long lashes fluttered open. Could she have communicated these erotic fancies? She turned away from his quizzically enquiring eyes and looked through the window, to catch her breath in delight.

Beneath the plane the waters of the Gulf had shallowed, and patches of what must be reefs provided the translucent water with an opportunity to show its versatility. From the deepest indigo blue to the palest aquamarine, the colour changed with the varying depths, and the view from the plane was a more exquisite blending of colours than any artist's palette could achieve.

'Look at it, Gabe,' she cried in delight. 'Just look at the colours.'

He came across to sit on the arm of her chair, and she welcomed his closeness. They would share this adventure as they had shared the magic of the beach at Mahabalipuram. If that was to be all, then it must be enough, but she hugged the excitement that the afternoon promised closely to herself.

'See the fine white line up ahead?' Gabe pointed to a corner of the window. 'That must be land.'

He was leaning against her, not with weight but with warmth, and she felt a quickening within herself as her body responded to his nearness. All the defences she had built up so carefully over the last twelve months were crumbling in the presence of this man.

'So the sleeping beauties have awoken!'

They turned from the window to see Nina in the door that lead through to the galley. 'So much for caviare! I was beginning to wonder if the champagne had been drugged.'

Gabe's hand had dropped unselfconsciously from the window to rest on Leith's shoulder, and she found, in its steady weight, a promise.

'We've been working too hard,' he explained with a rueful grin. 'I don't remember finishing the champagne.'

'You didn't,' Nina told him. 'I had to take both your glasses out of your hands before you spilled them all over the good carpet! Now, if you'll leave that woman alone and return to your seat, we'll be landing in about ten minutes.'

If Leith expected Gabe to be discomfited by Nina's suggestive remark she was mistaken.

'It'll be hard,' he said lightly, giving Leith's shoulders a squeeze and dropping a quick kiss on the top of her head, 'but you're the boss. I know the view won't be as good from my window.'

'We'll circle,' Nina responded firmly, pretending she hadn't understood him. 'Seriously, though, you'll soon see the city and the airport, which is built out into the sea. Our normal approach is from the Gulf, but Nate's going to take you for a bit of a joy-ride, and will circle out over the desert so you have some idea what's outside the strange oasis that's Abu Dhabi.'

While she was speaking the tiny white line had broadened. Leith could see the bright whiteness of the sand where the runways pushed out into the clean, clear water, and the pattern of high-rising buildings that denoted the city behind it.

Nina disappeared, and Leith lost herself in the magic

of discovery as she watched, entranced, the city passing beneath them, and the red-gold sands of the desert stretching endlessly to the horizon.

The plane flew in a low, sweeping arc, and the afternoon sun caught the city, lighting the glass in the tall buildings, seeking out golden domes on the Muslim temples that nestled alongside the Western architecture.

'Isn't it fantastic?' she said happily as she turned impulsively to Gabe. 'I'm so glad you decided to come.'

'Even if it's only for the money?' he teased.

'Bother the money. I'd work for nothing if people kept flying me to exciting places.'

'Would you, Leith?'

She looked away from the fast-approaching airport to study his face. There seemed to be more than one question in his words.

'Well, not forever, maybe,' she granted, 'but certainly on an occasional basis. India's wonderful——'

'In spite of the hours you work, and the heat and the horror of those people's faces?'

'Yes!' The single word carried a great conviction. 'To tell you the truth, Gabe, I don't think about work in terms of hours any more. If there's something I have to do, I do it. Times on and times off are very irrelevant, aren't they?'

'Only until you drop from exhaustion! That's when you remember why normal hospitals have rosters!'

There was a slight jarring through the body of the plane as the wheels touched down, then the muted roar of the engines as they went into reverse to slow the lumbering giant.

As silence descended, Nina reappeared.

'There's a car to meet you. It will take you straight to the hospital.'

'Is the lad still in hospital? I understood that the accident was some time ago, and I was here to patch up the scars.'

Gabe looked as disconcerted as he sounded, and Leith realised that the short sleep he had snatched on the flight was not nearly enough to make up for all the hours he had missed.

Nina chuckled at his dismay.

'The accident was weeks ago, but they have taken him back to the hospital this morning so you can operate this afternoon.'

'That's ridiculous. What if I'd had half a bottle of that champagne?'

Gabe was gathering their belongings as he spoke, picking up Leith's small overnight bag as well as his own.

'I wouldn't have served it,' she told them with a cheeky smile. 'In the Arab World most questions are answered with the word "*Inshallah*" or "as God wills", and we Westerners tend to think it denotes a mighty patience.'

'And you're saying it doesn't?' Leith asked. 'It certainly does in India. The phrasing is different, but it's the belief of the people that gives them their ability to wait.'

'Ah,' said the American girl, 'you're talking about the ordinary people. I wonder if the maharajas showed the same patience, or if they were more like our noblemen.'

'Will they really expect Gabe to operate this afternoon? Have they any idea how long a delicate graft operation could take?'

'I honestly don't know,' confessed Nina, 'but, knowing the system, I would expect so. You're only here for two days, I believe, and if he operates today he can check on the patient before we fly you back tomorrow evening.'

'But that's absurd. Why should he be rushed into it?' Leith argued.

'It'll be OK, Leith,' Gabe interrupted her, his eyes sparkling with amusement as he listened to her heated defence of himself. 'I have all the notes and pictures of the wound from the family's physician, and I think it will only be a flap, not a graft.'

'It's still too much to expect you to fly all this way then operate immediately,' she muttered mutinously.

'Perhaps the champagne *was* drugged!' he said, laughing at her dismay. 'Just look on the bright side——'

'Bright side?' she echoed explosively, unreasonably upset that their 'adventure' should begin like this.

'Yes,' he persuaded. 'It means we'll have the whole day tomorrow, apart from a brief hospital visit, to do some sightseeing.'

'Having flown over this town, there's nothing but desert to see anyway!'

She knew she was behaving ungraciously, but did not seem able to stop it, the disappointment she felt still raw and painful.

'Can you drive a boat, Gabe?' Nina was ushering them towards the now open door as she asked the unexpected question.

'All Queenslanders can drive boats,' he responded with a mock-pomposity that drew a reluctant smile from Leith. 'Why? Does the hospital flood?'

He's joking like this to cover my bad behaviour,

Leith thought, but the thought made her feel even worse. An eagerly anticipated afternoon and evening exploring this new city together had been abruptly taken from them, and he did not seem in the least upset.

Nina and Gabe were still talking, but she was too lost in her own disappointment to follow the conversation. She climbed carefully down the steps of the plane, registering the hot air that felt dry and prickly against her skin, after the moist heat of India. Without waiting for Gabe, she climbed into the back of the Mercedes that stood at the bottom of the gangway.

The driver hurried to relieve Gabe of their bags, stowing them in a boot that would hold a small elephant. Nina waited with Gabe by the gangway until Nate brought the instrument case down to the car. Over the hum of the air-conditioning, Leith could not distinguish their words, although they parted with the word 'tomorrow'.

'Were you arranging our flight back?' she asked him as he sank into the soft leather seat beside her a little later.

Her voice was flat. The magic seemed to have gone out of the day, and even Gabe's presence beside her as they sped through the modern city failed to rekindle the enthusiasm she had lost.

'No,' he answered, his face turned to the windows as if fascinated by the bright gardens they were passing.

Was that all he was going to say?

Looking across at the bit of profile she could see, she wondered if he was teasing her. Was it a smile that tugged at his lips?

More likely a twitch from exhaustion, she thought

crossly, unable to shrug off the depression that had settled on her spirits like a damp cloud.

The car slid to a silent halt at the doors of a massive new building, and a uniformed porter stepped forward to open the door.

'Back to work, Sister Robinson,' Gabe said brightly, and she glared furiously at him, her disappointment turning to anger, directed now at Gabe, who was docilely accepting the demands of this family.

'Anything for money, eh, Gabe?' she responded bitterly as she followed him through the doors and entered a world that was as familiar as her own home.

She fell into her role of assistant easily, nodding when Gabe performed introductions, but remaining quietly in the background, and following him with due subservience as he was led to the young man's room.

'You are most welcome, Dr Vincent.' A tall figure, robed in white, greeted Gabe as he entered the large room. In faultless English he performed the introductions. 'This is my brother, and our family physician——' he murmured their names to Gabe '—and my son, Aziz.' He waved his hand towards the bed.

Leith's eyes had been on the slight figure perched on the side of the bed since they entered the room. He seemed about thirteen, a boy-man, showing a bravado that was not reflected in his eyes.

Gabe moved confidently towards the bed, shaking hands with the lad, then saying, 'Do you understand English?'

The boy nodded, and Gabe continued, 'Well, let's see what damage you've done to yourself.'

He tilted the boy's face to the light, and immediately the angry red scars of the wound became visible.

'Fooling around, were you?' he asked nonchalantly,

then grinned at the boy's confirming nod. 'It could have been worse. Plenty of kids only learn to treat guns seriously when one of their mates is killed.'

Aziz nodded earnestly again, and a flicker of movement behind her caused Leith to half turn, to see the three white figures all nodding and whispering, as if giving a seal of approval to both Gabe and his words.

She turned back to Gabe, who caught her eye... and winked! She couldn't believe his attitude. She might have calmed down a little since she'd entered the familiar environs of a hospital and resumed the cloak of Sister Robinson, but her unreasonable disappointment still stung like a raw graze.

'You will tell us what you intend doing?'

It was the first man who spoke—obviously the boy's father—and Gabe moved towards them, speaking quietly. Leith caught the word 'flap' and was relieved that the boy would not have to undergo a graft, with all the painful preparation, and the subsequent scarring from a donor site as well.

He looked scared, poor kid, she thought, and moved towards the bed to stand beside him. Why wasn't his mother here? Her resentment at these men began to build again.

As if sensing her quick anger, the boy asked anxiously in clear but accented English, 'Will it be bad? What will he do?'

She reached out to take his hand, patting it reassuringly.

'It's not serious at all. What do you know already?'

She had always found that patients liked to air their knowledge, and the fact that professionals took time to listen often gave them confidence.

'Our doctor told me they will take a piece of skin

from my leg and put it on my face.' He paused for a long moment then continued, 'My brothers and cousins all tease me. They say I will grow leg hair on my face instead of face hair!'

'It just shows how silly they are,' Leith assured him quickly, understanding the confusion that was causing his anxiety. 'We hardly ever put leg hair on faces, and certainly never on a face as handsome as yours.'

She saw a glow of gratitude in his doe-shaped eyes, and felt a gentle return of pressure from the fingers that lay in hers. Anxious to complete her task of reassurance, she rushed on, 'Did you know that skin grows so quickly, we can take it from the same place every few weeks? But that's for people who need many grafts, like burn patients we are treating in India.'

'Where do you take skin from to put on faces?'

She had caught his interest now and intended to hold it.

'Mostly from around other parts of your head. You feel around behind your ear—there's skin there we can use, and all the skin on your neck and under your chin.'

The boy looked at her in surprise, then curiously felt his face, seeking confirmation of her words. The murmuring voices continued behind her.

'What is the doctor telling my father?'

Leith was wondering that herself. With patients of this age—or even younger—the procedure was usually explained to them first, or they were included in the explanation given to the family.

'He is telling him what he will do. Later he will tell you, but I'm pretty certain that what he's saying is that you won't need a graft at all. He can patch you up with what is called a "flap".'

Aziz pulled a face. 'That sounds worse,' he muttered.

'Yes, but it's an easier operation, and it will work far better. As well as growing fast, skin is very elastic.'

'It would have to be or fat people would burst.' He laughed at his own joke and Leith smiled, knowing that he was now relaxed enough for his normal nature to be asserting itself.

'That's right. So what Gabe—Dr Vincent—will probably do is cut away where the scars are and pull the skin from beside your ear here——' she moved her finger down his cheek '—forward across to here near your mouth, and fix it neatly there.'

The boy followed her description with his fingers.

'So I won't have a scar at all?' he asked quickly.

'Only a very faint and manly one that will make your face more interesting, and far more attractive.'

Gabe had moved silently to stand behind her, and she started at the sound of his voice.

'Like Sister Robinson's,' he went on, reaching out to take Leith's chin and turn it towards Aziz. 'See how this little scar here makes her more beautiful.'

His fingers traced the tiny cicatrice, and she trembled at the intimacy of his touch.

'Yes, that's a great scar,' Aziz agreed, excited now by the prospect. 'How did you get yours, Sister?'

'It was an accident!' she answered briefly, hiding the flaring panic that she felt at the memory. She stepped backwards, away from the boy, away from Gabe. . .

'I think Sister Robinson explained what we'll do. Is it OK with you if we go ahead now?'

At least Gabe was treating Aziz as a person as well as a patient, but, even accepting different customs, surely his mother should be here?

She looked at the three men, but all eyes were on

Gabe as his fingers probed the soft tissues of the boy's face.

'Because it's on your face, you'll have a general anaesthetic, but it will only be a light one, and you'll feel fine when you wake up. You won't have to stay in hospital, but will have a dressing over your face for a few days. Any questions?'

'No, sir,' the boy responded shyly, his eyes seeking Leith for reassurance.

'Then let's go!'

Gabe nodded to the men, and one — the physician, Leith presumed — led the way out of the room and down the sparkling passageway, past the doors of a small operating-theatre that was already set up to receive them, and into an ante-room.

Leith was relieved to see that the anaesthetist was in the regulation white of most hospitals and the nurses were in regular uniforms.

As the staff fussed around Aziz, preparing him for the operation, she was led into a spacious scrub-room where she changed into a waiting gown, and was assisted to scrub up and don her gloves.

The young nurse was swift and silent, as if overwhelmed by the magnitude of the occasion. Those bulky men in their snow-white robes and concealing head-dress would be enough to intimidate anyone, Leith thought ruefully.

Ushered through another door into the theatre, she found that the anaesthetist had already inserted a drip into the back of Aziz's slim hand. Gabe nodded to her, and she waited for her customary professional calm to take over, but, although she moved to the trolley and began her check with competence, the warring tension inside her did not diminish.

If anything the turmoil she felt was exacerbated by the closeness of the theatre, where Gabe's presence was an almost tangible force. She watched his gloved fingers as they marked the scarred area of the tanned cheek... Her eyes clouded and her mind slipped away into a fantasy land where none could follow.

'I'll close with those mini-staples, I think, Sister. They'll hold more firmly than steri-strips or sutures.'

She looked up at Gabe as she passed the machine with its tiny stainless steel staples already inserted. He winked again, success obvious in his shining eyes, and she felt a surge of relief. Her mind had been wandering throughout the entire operation, but her body must have responded automatically to his needs.

The phrasing of the thought shook her and she felt hot colour staining her face as she admitted the path those wayward notions had taken. It was a good thing he wasn't a mind-reader, she thought as she walked towards the door that led back to the changing-room.

'I'll see you soon,' he murmured, his hand resting briefly on her shoulder as he spoke the words close to her ear.

And don't read anything into that, she told herself firmly. You're so mixed up at the moment that you're likely to make a complete fool of yourself.

'The driver will take us to the hotel, where, so I'm told, dinner awaits us,' Gabe greeted her as she emerged a short time later in the passageway. He was standing with the other doctor, discussing dressings and antibiotics, but he smiled warmly at her as he spoke.

The sight of his tall, solid body and smiling face sent

her blood singing through her veins. Did he feel the ruthless intensity of the attraction that she felt, or could it be one-sided?

The kisses they had exchanged were hardly a test—tentative exploratory moves, nothing more! Yet she could not be in his presence without feeling a palpable excitement between them. Could he also feel it?

She followed the two men out of the building to the car—like a good Arab wife, she thought mischievously.

'Congratulations, Sister, you are an excellent theatre nurse.' The Arab, whose name remained a mystery, bowed slightly to her and opened the car door for her. 'I hope you enjoy the rest of your stay in my country.'

'Thank you,' she responded politely. 'I hope I will too.'

There was a depth of feeling in the words, but she was beyond analysing herself any further! Tiredness had begun to catch up as the let-down following the operation took over from the heady pleasure of another success.

'The day's nearly over, little one.'

He had used that term before—was it an endearment? It certainly made her feel cherished and protected—rare emotions for someone usually regarded as competent and self-sufficient!

Gabe leaned towards her in the car, his hand stretching out to stroke her short, silky hair, lifting the soft strands in his fingers, then letting them drop.

'It's nearly midnight, Indian time,' he explained, 'so you've reason to feel a bit washed out. We'll eat then sleep——'

'That's all I seem to do these days—sleep and eat, with work thrown in for variety.' Her voice was tetchy, but she knew that he was right. She was tired now that she had relaxed—but too tired for a possible dalliance with this attractive man?

'Ah,' he whispered softly, 'all that is about to change.'

His hand slipped from her head, trailing down her neck to rest on her shoulder. He pulled her over to lie against his body, and his lips moved against her tousled hair.

'Because tomorrow, my lovely Leith, we are going to run away—just you and I—and have a whole day all to ourselves.'

Her heart was thudding against her ribcage just lying this close against him, and the suggestiveness in his voice took her breath away.

'And it's no good asking for any details,' he continued before she could find her voice, 'because it's a special surprise just for you. A reward for being such a great nurse!'

'Is that all I am?' she asked bleakly, her ardour suddenly cooled by his final words.

'Why, of course,' he said, pushing her away a little so that his mocking eyes could look directly down into her perturbed ones. 'A very beautiful great nurse,' he added, and his mouth came gently down to seal his words with a promise of a kiss, a touching of flesh so light that it might not have happened, had not Leith's thirsting lips burned as if branded.

'We seem to have missed all the sights of Abu Dhabi.' Leith straightened up as the car slid to a halt outside what looked like a very sumptuous hotel, her light remark masking the depth of her feelings.

Climbing out of the car, she eyed the marble-lined lobby doubtfully.

'We should have brought more luggage,' Gabe joked

as he handed their two overnight bags to the porter and followed the driver to the reception desk.

'I should have worn my mink!' Leith responded, looking around the opulent elegance with awe as the formalities were attended to.

'You look perfectly charming, and would fit in anywhere,' said Gabe consolingly. 'We are obviously very important guests, from all the bowing and scraping that's going on over there, so we shall just act as if we stay in five-star hotels every day of the week.'

'Five-star? You must be joking. The Sheraton and the Mirage back home are five-star. This place must be about twenty-star!'

'Whatever it is, we might as well enjoy it,' Gabe answered, taking her arm and leading her towards the lift as a small retinue of hotel staff ushered them forward.

The lift rose in discreet silence, and opened into an ornately decorated foyer. A key was inserted in a lock and, with a flourish of arms and many polite bows, they were shown into a beautiful room that outdid even the luxury of the plane.

Furnished with antiques, or excellent replicas, in the style of Louis XIV, it delighted the senses. Beautifully arranged flowers reflected their colours in gilded mirrors, and a gold and crystal chandelier lit the room with a sparkling softness.

'Dare we sit on these chairs?' Leith whispered, eyeing their delicate legs before measuring Gabe's bulk with a teasing eye.

'There must be beds; maybe we can sit on them.'

'It is a suite, sir,' explained an underling, opening a door, to show a bedroom, complete with a four-poster bed, hung with rich blue and green brocades.

'Not quite meant for sitting on,' Leith murmured.

'With another bedroom over there.' The manager waved his arm across the room, and another lackey moved to open a door that led into a similarly decorated bedroom, different only in the colours of the furnishings, these being reds and pinks.

'There's always the loo, I suppose.'

'There's a bathroom off each bedroom, sir.'

The manager had caught at least one of Gabe's muttered words. 'And now, if you will excuse me, I will arrange for your dinner to be sent up. Do you wish to see our menu or will you leave it to the chef?'

Gabe looked at Leith, raising an eyebrow in silent interrogation.

'I'm too tired, and I think too hungry, to even attempt to read a menu.' She smiled at the manager. 'We'll stick with the chef,' she said.

He acknowledged her words with a slight nod, but turned to Gabe for confirmation.

'Is that what you wish, sir?' he asked politely. He might deal with women when he had to, but when a man was present all his instincts and upbringing forced him to heed the man.

'Of course,' Gabe replied, less aware than Leith of the subtle differences in this foreign culture.

'It will be served in half an hour, if that is suitable.'

The men began bowing their way towards the door, and Leith was amused to see Gabe responding with a slight bending from the waist as he said, 'That's great,' and followed them across the room to shut the door with a quiet emphasis behind their departing backs.

Leaning his bulk against the door, he surveyed the room once again, his eyes finally coming to rest on Leith.

'Want to toss for bedrooms, or shall we share?'

CHAPTER SEVEN

GABE'S question left Leith breathless for the second time in less than an hour, and she looked up at him to gauge his mood. His eyes were twinkling at her, blue lights alive behind his thick tangle of lashes.

'Pink for girls and blue for boys,' she said quickly, collecting her small bag and retreating across the room before he could reply.

The bathroom was as elegantly opulent as the rest of the suite, but there were delights awaiting her that she had never savoured before.

Set in a row along a low cabinet, pristine in their newness, was a range of toiletries that Leith had only read of. They were all Chanel, but, while she recognised the well-known Number Five, Number Nineteen was new to her and she had only heard of Cristalle and Coco. Choosing Coco because she liked the packaging, she split the wrapper that bound the little parcel and found bath oil and salts, soap, deodorant, body lotion, hand lotion, dusting powder, moisturising cream and eye cream—something for every bit of her body, all perfumed with the same subtle fragrance.

'Well, I hope it's subtle,' she told her reflection as she poured bath oil into the huge bath. 'Poor Dr Vincent will be overwhelmed if it isn't!'

She revelled in the luxury of the deep, hot, scented water, her vacillating thoughts dismissed as she gave herself up to the indulgence of the moment. Steam rose around her, and she lathered the softly scented soap all over her body, delighting in its creamy richness, then sank beneath the water, watching the bubbles float to the surface, their delicious perfume drifting intoxicatingly into the moist air.

A tentative tap on the door brought her back to reality.

'Dinner will be arriving shortly, and I've found the champagne.'

Gabe's voice and growing pangs of hunger enticed her out of her watery delight, and she dabbed herself dry on the thick fluffy towels before smoothing more of the hotel's beauty products over her slim body.

The lingering perfume filled her with a heady joy, and she felt sensuously alive, aware of every fibre of her being.

'I should be preparing to slip between satin sheets,' she told her flushed reflection, pulling on the thick towelling robe that hung in the bathroom.

Safely enveloped in its voluminous folds, she made her way into the sitting-room, where she found Gabe, similarly attired, staring with bemusement at the array of silver-covered dishes that were spread on a table in front of him.

'It just appeared,' he said in mock-dismay, waving his hand about helplessly. 'Here, have some champagne to give you the strength to cope with all of this!'

He lifted an opened bottle, frosted with ice, out of a silver bucket, and poured her a glass. She walked around the table, lifting the silver covers to examine the chef's selection and wonder at the diversity of the food.

'Here's to us!' Gabe handed her the glass and raised it in a smiling salute. She raised her glass in a silent toast, but as her eyes met his she felt a languorous ease sweep over her body, and was lost in a situation which she could no longer control.

'Sit down, Leith.'

He spoke sharply, and she found her legs folding beneath her as if all her energy was suddenly draining away.

'Have a sip of champagne—it will revive you—while I put some of this food on a plate.'

'I should be looking after you,' she protested weakly.

'Don't be silly. I should have insisted they feed us before that operation. Just because my system has adjusted to long hours without food. . .'

He paused as he carefully selected small servings of food from the different dishes, adding tempting titbits about the edges.

'You've been looking pale and tired lately as it is, then to put you through a marathon like today. . .'

Again his voice faded. He placed the plate on the table in front of her and hovered anxiously above her. His hand reached out and a slender finger touched her face.

'There's a little colour coming back into your cheeks,' he said with rough concern.

'Soaking too long in the hot bath,' she told him lightly, afraid that he might guess the strange effect he had on her. 'The champagne revived me!'

'In that case, you can prove it to me—eat!' he commanded.

She smiled up at him, putting down her half-empty glass and selecting a fork from the array of cutlery set before her.

'Only when you do.' She shook the fork at him in a mock-admonition, then began to sample the various delights he had set before her.

'Oh, Gabe, it's wonderful!' The delicately spiced food warmed her body and restored her equilibrium, while the champagne sent her spirits soaring.

Across the table, Gabe eyed her critically, before smiling genially at her.

'It seems to have done the trick, anyway,' he said. 'For a moment there I thought you were going to pass out on me.'

'And you'd have had to eat all the food so as not to offend our hosts.'

'I'd have had to eat alone, which would have been much harder.'

He spoke softly, but the sincerity—the suggestion— in his voice was unmistakable, and she found herself trembling. What did he want of her, this aloof, contained man?

She dropped her eyes to her plate as she tried to untangle her thoughts and emotions. She knew that her own response to him was the result of a powerful physical attraction. She wondered if the concern she felt for his well-being, and the constant nagging need to be near him, were symptoms of love.

'Do you want to try any of the sweets?'

His question interrupted her thoughts and her eyes flew to meet his—dark flashes of blue, all emotion hidden by his long lashes.

'I think I've done well!' she admitted, pushing aside a nearly empty plate and draining the champagne from her glass.

He stood up and came around the table, clearing her plate away from in front of her and filling her glass. Her body throbbed its awareness of him.

'Shall we finish our drinks on the terrace? Abu Dhabi by night awaits you.'

He gestured towards the curtained windows, and she rose to follow him more slowly, her mind still trying to rationalise her tumultuous feelings.

She had thought she knew what love was once before, but her emotions had betrayed her. She tried to remember how she had felt with Mark, but couldn't recall this mixture of need and anxiety that Gabe engendered in her.

Then the magic of the terrace took her breath away.

'Oh, Gabe,' she breathed.

'You'll have to stop saying "Oh, Gabe" like that, my little one. It fills me with an irresistible urge to take you in my arms and hear you breathe it again into my ear.'

His arms encircled her from behind, and one hand reached out to take her glass and place it carefully on a small table.

'Now come and see the sights before we forget why we're here.'

With arms still enfolding her closely, he ushered her forward to the wide balustrade where huge urns held sweetly scented plants—night-flowering jasmine among them, she thought as she recognised the heady perfumes.

'Lights of Abu Dhabi,' he whispered in her ear, his warm breath sending shivers of delight down her spine.

The city sparkled beneath them, coloured lights reflecting in the water that seemed to encroach on the city, and bright flares lighting up the arched façades of so many of the buildings where East and West melded in a uniqueness that Leith found fascinating.

'And lights of the desert.'

Gabe pulled her body back to rest against his, so that her head tilted upwards. His arms tightened about her waist and she felt her breasts swell with desire as they felt the warmth of his hands—so close!

Above them, the heavens were ablaze with a mass of twinkling lights as the clear desert air revealed the true beauty of the stars.

For long moments they stood silent, steeped in the magic of the night, wrapped in the enchantment of their adventure.

Finally Leith stirred, and the slight movement of her body, held so closely against Gabe's, brought an unmistakable response from him.

Slowly he turned her towards him, and looked down into eyes that reflected the starlight.

'I love you, Leith Robinson,' he said quietly.

'You don't have to say that, Gabe.' She held him close and breathed the words against his neck, her lips feeling the blood pulsing strongly through his veins, tasting the maleness of his skin.

'Why not, little one?' he asked her with infinite tenderness. His lips sought and found hers so that she felt the words just millimetres from her mouth, and she shivered with the longing to savour him. Desperately she strained upwards, finding the mouth that tantalised her, and pressed her soft lips to his as if seeking succour and release.

His response was immediate and his mouth ground against hers with a desperation that matched her own. His tongue sought entry and her lips parted willingly, as if to drink in the essence of this man, the very core of his being.

The balmy night air held them wrapped in its embrace as they stood, swaying slightly, locked by a passion for too long denied, learning the secrets of each other that words would never reveal.

How long they remained there she would never know; but she would remember forever the desolate feeling of loss that swept over her as Gabe raised his head and breathed deeply for a moment before his eyes returned to her face, tracing the features in the starlight as if seeking to imprint them in his mind forever.

'Why not, Leith?'

So lost was she in the sensuous dream he had created that the question had no meaning, and she gazed up at him, seeking for a gleam in the dark shadows that held his eyes, or a clue in the beautiful moulding of his swollen lips.

'Is love off limits?' he asked. 'Does it frighten you?'

He spoke lightly, his strong hands holding her with a gentle reassurance, but she felt there was a depth of hidden meaning behind the words, and the turmoil within her deepened. Her lashes dropped to hide her thoughts — heaven forbid that he should start to read them!

He would wait forever for an answer, she knew that, so she had to find one.

To commit herself to love with Gabe was to invite hurt of a magnitude that made her previous experience seem trivial. Yet she wanted him with an urgency that was distracting her more and more each day.

Tread lightly, Leith, she warned herself as she raised her eyes once more to his face, and saw the jutting bones outlined so starkly against the starry sky.

'Love seems to have lost its meaning, Gabe,' she replied. 'It's a word used too lightly, to cover up for other words like attraction and desire.'

'Oh, I desire you too, my sweet; make no mistake about that!'

He pulled her close, as if to prove his words, and she

felt the tight hardness of his arousal. His head bowed towards her again and his lips traced a path across her forehead, lingering on each eyelid, then trailing down her cheek to tease at the corner of her lips, to nuzzle against her chin and send tremors of delight through her body as his tongue teased erotically at her ear.

Again he drew away, and she strained to recapture his lips, but they were moving against her hair as he said, 'But there's love as well, Leith.'

He said it with such finality that she was forced to believe him. For whatever reason—probably sheer propinquity—he fancied he had fallen in love with her. Well, that's OK, she thought, because love doesn't last. Her heart beat uncomfortably fast as she forced herself to accept this dubious statement.

'For some people, maybe,' she said, the anguish of her words hidden behind a light tone and downcast eyes.

'But not for Sister Robinson?' he mocked. 'Let's see about that, shall we?'

His tormenting lips sought hers once more, but this time they did not tease or tantalise. This time his mouth claimed hers to burn against it with a flaming hunger that seemed to sear her through to her heart.

His arms moved against the thick fabric of her towelling robe as he gathered her into his arms. Then, with his mouth still plundering hers, he lifted her as lightly as he would a child, and carried her through the open doors to his bedroom.

'Tell me you don't want me.' He breathed the words hoarsely against her lips as he bent to rest her, with infinite care, on the snowy sheets of the turned-back bed.

'I can't,' she whispered back, her hands reaching up as if to drag him down against her body.

'Well, that's a start,' he murmured, his voice deep and smoky with desire.

The words washed sibilantly around her, but her body lay as if drugged.

Gabe's hands traced a fiery path down her cheek, dropping lower to feel the contours of her neck and tease at the delicate bones of her shoulders, while his burning eyes held hers with a mesmeric intensity.

Reaching the lapels of her loose robe, he traced their path, one finger trailing on her satiny skin as he followed the thick material down to her waist and undid the knot that held it closed. With great deliberation he pushed the robe apart, his gaze finally leaving her face to take in the beauty of her naked body.

She saw the heated flash of desire in his eyes as they lingered on her taut breasts, which yearned towards him with a will of their own. Her arms reached up again to pull him down, to hold him close and still her desperate longings.

'Oh, no, my little one,' he said softly, and, catching her hands, he pushed them back on to the bed, then knelt astride her thighs.

His body was close, yet not touching hers, his knees pinning her hands so that she lay beneath him like a helpless suppliant.

'I love you, Leith Robinson,' he repeated, and the words became an incantation of desire.

'I love you, love you, love you.'

His hands moved as he chanted softly, teasing at her skin with such delicate sensitivity that her body arched towards him, and her breathing quickened as she fought for some control over the flames he was igniting inside her.

His fingers teased and fondled at her breasts, circling her rosy nipples until they prickled into painful points of desire, and her body twisted as it sought relief.

She watched his face, so intent, his body under complete control while he teased hers to the edge of madness. She felt his hands leave her aching breasts and track down her sensitised skin, caressing her slender waist, and lingering lovingly on her jutting hipbones, as if seeking to know her through their touch.

They teased among the soft hair that protected her hot, sweet wetness, and she cried out for him to ease the pulsing, tortuous desire that quivered through her body. Her cry went unheeded, and those roaming, questing hands slid slowly back up her body to circle once again around her breasts and brush, with a feather-light touch, the hard nubs he had aroused.

'Say you love me, Leith.'

His eyes lifted momentarily to hers, the message he had ceased repeating written clearly there for her to read. Then his head dropped and his mouth closed on her breast, his tongue probing, his lips sucking, his teeth nipping at the delicate tissues until she moaned aloud and cried his name and begged for him to take her.

'Say you love me,' he commanded fiercely, his heightened desire obvious in his ragged, gasping breath. 'Say it, Leith,' he insisted, raising his head to look into her yearning eyes.

'No!' she muttered defiantly, determined not to give in to him in everything. She would not—could not—deny him her body, but she would never say the words he wanted to hear.

He held her desperate gaze for a moment longer, then, with great deliberation, lowered his head until his lips met her other breast.

She whimpered softly as he continued his electrifying assault, but this time the rhythm was different. Her whole being quivered with an urgency that she had never felt before as her body twisted and writhed under a touch that ravished her senses.

As if seeking to still her wild, abandoned movements, he lowered his body to rest against hers, his knees still supporting his weight as they kept her arms imprisoned on the bed.

She felt his hardness rub against her, while his lips and hands continued the sweet torture on her breasts, and she cried out for relief as the tension inside her mounted to a molten surge of heat.

'Please, Gabe. . .' she pleaded, her breath coming in hot gasps as she fought for control over her craving, yearning body.

'Say you love me!'

His voice was harsh now—demanding—as if the last shreds of his determination were all that held him under such iron control.

She saw the heated flush that darkened his skin, and the feverish glitter in his eyes as he sought her reply, but she could not give in. Not even to satisfy the demons that were driving her into a frenzy could she lay bare her soul to this man. Not yet, and maybe not ever!

She shook her head wearily, moving it from side to side like an automaton, and tears welled up in her eyes and slid slowly across her lower lashes and down across her temples.

'Don't cry, my darling, my little one!'

His voice was rough with a penitence she had never heard from a man before, and he gathered her up in his arms, moving to lie beside her while his lips sought the moisture of her tears.

All composure gone, he gentled her with hands of love, desperately caressing and comforting her as he cradled her in his arms.

Again she found herself responding. The searing, flaming hunger that had died down with his insistent demands began to flicker back to life. Her fingers sought the silken warmth of his skin as they pushed aside his robe and held his firm, warm bulk close against her. Free now to rove, to do their own exploring, her hands traced the line of his backbone, feeling the interplay of muscle and bone, the gentle inward curve of his waist and the swelling firmness of his buttocks.

'I love you, Leith,' he breathed against her ear as she held him close, feeling his body fit itself to hers as if they were two parts of a whole being, now complete at last.

With a gentle cadence they found each other, giving and taking such pleasure that Leith would always remember the night with the soft cries of their eager loving echoing in her ears.

She woke refreshed, exulting in the warmth of the body that pressed against her, cradling her in arms that were heavy with sleep. The sensual pleasure of skin on skin spread through her and she rubbed herself sensuously against her lover, feeling the wiry hair that matted his chest prickling against her back.

I shouldn't wake him, she told herself, knowing how little sleep he was getting these days, but her movements must have already aroused him, for she felt his body quickening against her, and she turned in his arms to mould herself tightly against him, seeking some oblivion of soul as she lost herself in his fierce possession.

'Good morning,' he greeted her some time later as she snuggled, flushed and breathless, against his chest.

She looked up to see his shining eyes looking down at her with such tender passion that her heart somersaulted within her and she felt as if she might melt away.

'A very good morning,' she affirmed, her eyes teasing at him as she tried to hide the feelings he had aroused.

'We've got to get up,' he said determinedly, holding her tightly in his arms and making no move to rise.

'Must we? Can't we stay here all day?'

'Don't tempt me, little witch!' He blew against her fine hair, and she could feel it lifting off her forehead.

'Can't we stay a little longer? We could sleep and——'

'I know what "and",' he interrupted, 'and we'd probably do more of that than sleep, but there's a new world waiting outside there, and we've one day to see it.'

'Blow seeing it,' Leith said gruffly, burrowing against his chest.

'Is this the girl who complained that we missed our sightseeing tour yesterday because some inconsiderate nobleman wanted us to operate?'

Gabe's voice sounded so young and carefree that it caught at Leith's heart-strings. Was it love, or simply a good night's sleep that had relaxed him like this? A shadowy doubt flitted across her mind, but she banished it immediately.

'Well,' she sighed, 'if we're going all practical I need a shower, and I think I might be hungry. Do you suppose if we rub one of the beautiful jars that are stuck on all the tables round this suite a genie might appear with coffee?'

With a quick hug Gabe released her, sitting up in the bed to gather her bathrobe off the floor and hand it to her.

'You have a shower, and I'll find the genie.'

He walked towards his bathroom, and her eyes, soft with the love she must hide from him, feasted on the long, clean lines of his naked back, tanned to where his slim hips were marked with the white line of his swimming-trunks. Long, lean legs, with muscled calves. . . She felt a fresh tremor of desire ripple through her.

She gathered up her robe and fled.

'Real coffee has just arrived, and you'll need a swimsuit.'

Hardly romantic, but intensely practical, Leith thought as she pulled on skimpy navy and white polka dot bikini pants. The cheeky bra top covered her breasts, but did something special to them, so that they curved voluptuously above the dark fabric.

Eyeing herself in the mirror, she gave a small nod of satisfaction, pleased with the sight the Gabe would see later.

How stupid, she thought immediately, shaking her head as she tied a long, softly gathered skirt of the same material around her slim waist. He's seen everything there is to see. And she blushed at the memory.

Reaching into her small bag, she found a sleeveless white camisole top that looked reasonably uncrushed, and pulled it on to cover her seductive top, completing her outfit with the short-sleeved navy and white striped blazer that she had worn on the flight the day before. Flat-heeled white sandals added a finishing touch to the picture as she pirouetted in front of the big mirror.

Quite a smart-looking 'sheila', she told her reflection, using the slang expression in an effort to calm her racing pulse and settle the hectic flush that glowed in her cheeks and shone in her eyes.

'Wow!' One word and the dancing gleam of appreciation told her all she needed to know, and her eyes left Gabe's face to scan his 'going out' clothes.

'We match,' she said in delight, taking in the dark blue knit shirt that clung to his broad shoulders and emphasised the bulge of his tanned biceps.

The shirt was tucked into white linen shorts that clung to his hips, emphasising their slimness and contrasting with the strength of his bare legs.

'I love you, Leith Robinson.' He echoed the words across the room at her, then came towards her and took her hands, to lead her out on to the balcony where breakfast and the sparkling city awaited her.

'Real coffee!' She breathed deeply, savouring the aroma and trying to behave as nonchalantly as possible, given that she had spent a night of fairly unbridled passion in the arms of this man, and was still trying to deny his declarations of love!

'And real croissants, and real Danish pastries, and real eggs, and real orange juice.' Gabe bowed her with a flourish to a chair. 'There's also fruit and sausages and some species of fish, and quite a lot of things I've never seen before.'

'Did you order all this lot?' she asked in amazement as she peered under the mass of silver covers that rivalled the setting of the previous evening's dinner.

'Of course not,' he said gravely. 'I merely lifted the phone and said, "Breakfast, please," and the genie did the rest.'

'Just coffee and croissants for me.' Leith reached out and selected a hot, buttery roll and peeled the lid off a tiny tub of raspberry jam. 'What bliss!'

She sipped at her coffee, then bit into the soft roll, delighting in its flaky freshness. Across the table Gabe was demolishing a plate of sausages and eggs, with various local delicacies added for flavour or interest.

She watched with intense fascination as his agile fingers moved above the plate, cutting, selecting, and finally conveying the chosen morsels to his mouth. Those pale lips parted, and Leith held her breath, drawn back into intimate memories of the night with such force that when Gabe looked across and met her eyes she felt a scarlet heat rush to her face.

'It's a good thing we'll be on our own for most of the day,' he said with a quiet humour as she bowed her head in confusion over her plate. 'I wouldn't like other people to read some of the thoughts that are written on your so expressive face, little one.'

She shook her head as if to clear it, and picked up her coffee-cup, trying to still her trembling fingers by cupping it between her hands.

'What are the plans?' she enquired politely, struggling to regain some composure.

'Bring your coffee over here and I'll explain.' He stood up, holding his coffee-cup, and motioned towards the edge of the balcony.

The city lay revealed beneath them like a contour

HEALING LOVE

map in a child's atlas. Directly below, a mosque, its golden onion dome glinting in the morning sun, sat against a backdrop of city buildings, a clutter of steel, glass and concrete.

Beyond this commercial heart stretched the houses, built in the unmistakable style of the architecture of the East—low, solid buildings washed in white or ochre, spreading in a suburban sprawl for miles. Strange-shaped domes or spires decorated the flat roofs, and delicate scalloped parapets guarded the sides. The thick fronds of date palms provided occasional breaks of green, and thorny-looking bushes straggled their trailing arms over low arches.

Here and there were gardens, bright with tropical flowers, flourishing with a vitality that belied their desert soil. Far into the distance her eyes picked out a long line of green, as if a road, leading out into the bare surrounding countryside, had been planted with trees.

'Well, what do you see?' Gabe asked, as her eyes scanned the fascinating scene beneath her.

'Buildings, houses, gardens, sand.'

'Nothing else?'

'Like what?'

She was uncertain of him in this teasing mood, although she was beginning to believe that this might be the real Gabe.

'Water, maybe?'

'Well, there's plenty of that. Strange, isn't it,' she mused, 'that this is a desert? Because there's no water, and yet the whole town is practically surrounded by the stuff.'

'Wrong sort of water, unfortunately.' Gabe agreed

with her. 'But it will do us. Now, Sister Robinson, what do you have when you put sand beside the water?'

'A beach! We're going to the beach?' The concept puzzled her. 'But it's all beach, isn't it?' she said slowly. 'Where the desert comes down to the water there must be beach, yet I've never thought of Arab countries as beachy sort of places. I mean, they're not usually considered as holiday resorts.'

'Not like Florida or the Seychelles or Cannes!' he teased.

'No,' she agreed, still doubtful. 'Is it safe?'

'Completely,' he assured her, coming close to take her cup and hold her lightly in his arms. 'Now shall we go?'

Blow in my ear and I'll follow you anywhere! In her mind she echoed a phrase her mother had often used, while her body tingled from his light embrace.

'I'll get my things.'

As they walked out of the hotel into the hot, dry air, a long, low American convertible slid to a halt in front of them, and a uniformed boy moved swiftly to open the door.

'To the British club, please, driver,' Gabe said with a laugh, and Leith was delighted to see Nate at the wheel.

'I thought I'd drive you over and introduce you to the boat. Your driver will be back on duty this afternoon,' he explained, adding with a grin, 'And now, lady and gentleman, sit back and enjoy a guided tour of Abu Dhabi.'

'The gardens are fantastic, Nate. I can't believe their richness and the colour of the flowers.' Leith looked about her in delight, her joy in Gabe's presence adding a radiance to the day.

'Tropical air and desalinated water, that's all it takes,' Nate told her.

'What a difference water makes,' she said, watching busy gardeners at work in the parks that lined the streets.

'What a difference oil makes, you mean!' Nate replied. 'It's the money from the oil that provides the miracles. It pays the Pakistani and Filipino workers who make the gardens possible, it pays to turn the salty water into fresh—it even pays to irrigate the trees that they are planting along the roads that cross the desert!'

'You're kidding?' Gabe said, disbelief in his voice.

'No joke! You should see the road to El Ain—one hundred and sixty miles of polythene pipe to drip water on the trees that line it. . .on both sides!'

'It's unbelievable after India,' Leith exclaimed, as they passed a camel sitting proudly at ease by the side of the road.

They whisked through streets that teemed with life as white- and black-clad figures went about their daily business. The road curved around towards the shore, and Leith was fascinated by the wooden fishing boats, with their high curving prows and short crossed masts from which tattered sails hung lifeless in the still air.

'What happens at the British club?' she asked quietly, her eyes still on the boats that dotted the blue waters.

'You'll find my speedboat there, on loan to you as a special favour for the day.'

Leith turned to Gabe.

'So that's what you and Nina were whispering about!'

'Merely arranging a beach for you, my heart.' Gabe

winked at her, as he did so often in theatre. 'We could loll around the pool at this club place they have, but Nate assures me that it's far better to take the boat.'

'Take the boat where?' she asked, puzzled by the idea.

'Along the coast a little way. There's actually hundreds of miles of beach for you to choose from, but I think you'll find a nice deserted patch of it pretty close to town,' Nate told her, while Gabe smiled at her confusion.

'It's like India, Leith,' he explained, 'a totally different culture. You know they frown on bare arms and legs, so imagine how your average Arab might feel about near-naked Westerners frolicking on his desert sands. It's really a courtesy on the part of the expatriates. They go away from the settlement so as not to offend their hosts.'

It was a magical day that would never—could never—be repeated. The land shelved steeply, enabling them to stay close in to the sandy shore. They followed the coast for about thirty minutes, then pulled in to unload the picnic packed by the hotel, and the towels and rugs left for them by Nate and Nina.

As if purified by the waters, the sand on the beach was crisp and white, darkening almost imperceptibly to the red-gold of the desert within sight of where they sat. Leith slipped out of her skirt and top, and started to rub sunscreen into her pale skin.

She felt Gabe's eyes following her fingers as they moved over her silken thighs and down the length of her legs, and the banked embers of their passion flared back into flickering life. How would she be able to work with him again if one glance could inflame her like this?

'Race you in,' she said suddenly, unable to bear the rising heat or her tortured thoughts.

The milky-blue water cooled and soothed her, and she swam and frolicked with a carefree delight that she thought she had lost forever.

Bother tomorrow, she thought. I'll have a wonderful today!

Then Gabe swam alongside her, his body slick and glistening, tempting her to touch and taste, to feel the strength of muscles beneath skin that rippled with vitality.

'I hope you're prepared for the consequences of all this licentious behaviour,' he told her as he nibbled at her ear, his body moving sensuously under her wandering hands.

'Not only prepared,' she gasped as his hands moved to free her breasts and his lips left her ear and trailed down along her neck to suck with tantalising tenderness at an erect nipple, 'but ready and waiting.'

She felt the rush of moisture released within her body as it cried out for his to satisfy her need, and a soft moan started deep in her throat as she felt his weight settle on her in the shallow water, his body fitting to hers in an age-old rhythm until all thought was suspended and they sought the joys their new-found knowledge of each other could provide.

Much later she lay back on the rugs among the scattered remains of their lunch, a towel loosely covering her nakedness and protecting her from the sun. Gabe sat above her, idly tracing the contours of her face with one long finger.

'Will you marry me?'

The question, coming so quietly, and so completely out of the blue, set her heart pumping furiously, and a hectic flush spread through her. But she knew the answer.

'No, Gabe. I'll have an affair with you, be your lover for a while, but I won't marry you.'

His finger continued on its exploratory way, teasing at her bones and fingering her skull. He had acknowledged her refusal with a nod, but did not comment, and she felt a fierce disappointment that he had not argued or pleaded with her—just a little.

Her eyes closed under the soothing finger, and she drifted into a dream. . .

'You've a beautiful face, Leith.' He spoke lightly, as if to erase any significance from their previous conversation. 'Structurally it's perfect.'

'No work for you to do on it?' she teased.

'No, my little one!'

His reply was soft, but, opening her eyes, she saw the relaxed muscles of his face tighten up again and his eyes cloud with some bitter memories.

'Tell me about Katherine,' she said, very quietly, aware of some hidden wound deep inside this man that would fester forever if not allowed out into the open to heal.

He turned away, to look out over the calm sea that shimmered under a molten sun.

'You knew her, knew that striking beauty that she had. I was overwhelmed by it, Leith. It was my business, and here was a woman who personified all that was perfect in it. But in the end—well. . .'

She waited for him to finish.

'I'm sure you've heard the stories.'

'I've heard so many stories that I stopped listening a

long time ago, Gabe,' she said doggedly, reaching up to turn his head back towards her. 'I want to hear your story.'

'Three years after we were married we found that she had leukaemia. I was determined we could beat it, and she underwent some frightful months of chemotherapy. She lost weight and, of course, lost her lovely hair.'

Leith's hand moved soothingly on his arm as he spoke, but she did not comment in case her words stopped the uneasy flow of his.

'She had a wig, hand-made,' he continued in a curiously detached voice. 'It looked so real! But her skin—she was so thin. . .'

'I can imagine,' Leith said softly, encouraging the remembrance.

'She went into remission, was really well, but she refused to go anywhere, refused to be seen—"with my face like this", she always said.'

He turned back from the sea, to look at her with blank eyes, and his hands reached out to pick up a twig that had found its way on to the rug. Her eyes followed his fingers, mesmerised as he twisted the stick in his hands, betraying the agitation that she thought he had lost.

'The specialist thought. . .'

'Tell me, Gabe.' She spoke steadily, but with a quiet insistence, convinced that there were words he had to speak before the ghosts of the past could be exorcised.

'He thought that she had lost all will to live because she believed she had lost her beauty. She was young, and had been healthy. She should have been able to fight it, but. . .'

'But she didn't want to?'

'That's what he said. It's what she said, too, when she begged me to agree to the operation, pleaded with me to help her get back the face she felt she'd lost. It was as if, without her face, she was nothing!'

There was a bitter, despairing anguish in his words, and he bent forward over his knees, his knuckles white as they broke the stick into minute pieces with his ceaselessly moving hands.

'We thought it might help!' His voice was a plea for understanding, but the rough, dry sobs that shook his frame affected Leith more deeply than his words.

She knew the rest, knew that the remission had ended and Katherine had died soon after the operation.

Her arms went around him, holding him close against her sun-warmed body while she rocked him gently, murmuring the meaningless soothing sounds of comfort.

'Professionally, I should have refused to help or advise her.' He said it with such cold conviction that she shivered.

'You agreed out of love, Gabe, and the final decision was hers, not yours!' she responded quickly, puzzled that he would judge his emotional actions or reaction by the harsh light of professional ethics.

'It was still wrong.'

He sees only black and white, she thought sadly. No shades of grey! What harsh rules to live by!

He must have sensed her slight withdrawal, for he turned and kissed her very softly on the cheek.

'Race you in!' he challenged, spent emotion dragging at his voice.

The face that lifted to hers was lined and weary, but his words told her that he had shrugged off the worst of his memories.

'I'll beat you,' she promised, thrusting aside her own disturbing thoughts.

She flung off the towel and flew across the hot sand. Gabe's story explained a lot, and any lingering doubts she had about this man she loved dissipated like the fine sprays of water that they splashed on the desert sand.

CHAPTER EIGHT

LEITH and Gabe returned to the hotel, tired and sandy, their ardour cooled by the turbulent emotions of the afternoon. A tender bond drew them close, holding them in a tighter thrall than even their shared passion had produced.

'The car will be back for you at seven,' Gabe told her, pushing her towards her unused bedroom. 'Have a shower, and order a light snack. There's plenty of time.'

'Gabe. . .?'

She turned to face him, but was unable to put into words all the things she wanted to say. She couldn't tell him how she felt, couldn't ask him what would happen tomorrow and the next day, couldn't predict with any certainty a future of any kind between them.

She only knew her part of things—knew that she was his. For as long as he wanted her, she would be there. But she also knew that she would not marry him and deny him the right to have children—nor tell him and force him to choose!

He looked down into her eyes as the worried shadows chased across them, then his arms came around her and held her close.

'We'll go back to India and finish the job that we set out to do,' he told her calmly, his hands fondling her tenderly. 'That's all we need to plan for now!'

She nodded her head, moving against him in confirmation of his words.

For a few moments longer they stood enjoying the contours of each other's bodies, until he pushed her slightly away and tilted her face up to his, so that she could see his blue eyes twinkling with a wry amusement.

'I do know this, little one,' he said with rueful candour. 'I am too old, and will be too busy and probably too tired, to conduct any clandestine hospital affairs.'

She had to chuckle! The image of this contained man creeping down the corridor to her room in the dead of night was one she could not believe, any more than she could see herself commuting to his hotel for the sake of physical release from sexual tension.

'You can laugh, you little witch, but I'll be tempted by the sight of you every day in that torture chamber you call a theatre! But I'll think of something,' he warned. 'Now get showered; I've got to leave.'

'You've got to leave?'

'I do have a patient to see,' he explained with a smile. 'Had you forgotten why we came?'

She blushed vividly, and he went on to explain.

'I spoke to his own physician this morning and all was well, but I must check the flap and leave some instructions.'

He kissed her softly on the top of her tousled head. 'So,' he continued, 'I'm having a quick shower, then going. There's also a little matter of money to be discussed with Aziz's father, so I'll go straight from my meeting with him to the plane.'

He held her close against him for a long moment, before pushing her towards the door.

She moved slowly, reluctant to be parted from him, reluctant to leave this dream world.

She knew that Gabe would cope. He was too professional to let his personal life interfere with the mass of work that lay ahead of him, and she hoped that she could match him in this regard. She shrugged her sandy shoulders.

Only time would tell! Then the lovely Indian word drifted into her mind—it would be 'Karma'—or even 'Inshallah'.

'Gabe's already here, and the boss is with him,' Nina greeted her when she arrived back at the airport. 'It seems they haven't finished their discussions, so he's coming with us.'

Leith was puzzled. Was Gabe angling for a job in the Emirates? She had heard that specialists could earn fabulous sums of money in the Arab countries.

'Are you afraid an extra passenger will spoil the flight back?' Nina asked seeing the frown that puckered Leith's brow.

Leith looked blankly at her, then realised what she was saying.

'Of course not. With my record, I'll be asleep by the time we gain whatever altitude Nate flies at.'

No, she thought, what teased at her mind was money. She had judged Gabe earlier for his money-hungry attitude. Now that she knew the man inside the surgeon's gown, the judgement she had made did not seem right. Yet he was deep in discussions with the nobleman, and what, besides money, could they be talking about?

She shook her head and climbed the steps into the spacious interior, nodding to the two men, who looked up as she entered.

A small table was fixed between them, littered with sketches and scraps of paper.

Against the soft murmur of their voices, she slept.

'Wake up, sleepyhead.'

Gabe's voice came into her dreams and she looked up as he gave her a quick squeeze on the shoulder before following the white-robed figure out of the plane.

'You're back in Madras,' Nina explained kindly, seeing Leith's drowsy confusion. 'The car's at the bottom of the steps, and the boss is still talking to Gabe. I rather gather he's going back to the hospital with you.'

They returned to chaos!

Mark met them on the veranda and was soon explaining things to Gabe, the white-robed watcher silent beside him. A number of outpatients had returned and been readmitted with infections on the donor sites, and a new graft was showing signs of coming unstuck. Leith had heard this much before Kala touched her arm.

'Will you come with me?' she asked quietly. 'There's something strange and I can't work it out.'

Leith looked at the other woman, noticing the deep purple shadows that gave her tired eyes a bruised look.

Quietly she dropped her bag and followed Kala down the corridor.

'It could be the dressings they've been using,' Leith said with conviction as she looked at the third infection site. 'The infection is such a regular shape, either square or rectangular. The skin around the wound looks just as bad.'

'But why just on the donor sites?' Kala had obviously been puzzling over the matter all day.

'Most of the sheet grafts are left uncovered, so we can watch for clots or infections, and the mesh grafts. . .'

She paused for a moment as she thought back to the theatre and the procedure they usually followed.

'They have a moist dressing,' Kala said quickly.

'Yes, and it's attached to the staples, so the patients wouldn't be changing it. It's got to be something to do with the dressings, Kala.'

She looked with concern at the patient, and noted the flush of fever and the rapid pulse throbbing in his thin neck.

'Did you keep any of them?' It was a chance, but she doubted it.

'No, they were all so bad they went straight into the incinerator bags. Could we have tested them?'

'It doesn't matter, Kala; we can run tests on the infection from the moisture that's seeping from the site. Perhaps Prakash or Mark has already done that.'

Kala nodded.

'Prakash sent specimens away this morning when he realised that the antibiotics were not affecting it at all.'

'Well, that's a start. What we can do is find out where those dressing came from.'

Kala looked puzzled.

'Surely from here,' she said quickly. 'We gave all the people spare dressings for their wounds before we sent them home.'

Gabe's head appeared round the door.

'Could you come along to the theatre and get scrubbed up immediately, please, Leith?'

She looked at him, surprised at the peremptory note in his voice, but her mind was still following another path.

'I'll be there shortly, Gabe,' she answered, almost absent-mindedly.

'I said immediately, Sister,' he responded shortly, and disappeared from view.

She shook her head, a puzzled frown deepening on her brow, but her mind returned to the problem confronting them.

'Talk to the patients, Kala, and find out if any of them used their own dressings, and, if so, where they got them.'

'I have already done that. They say they use ours, but——'

'If you're not sure, ask them again, or speak to their relatives. Then check the dates these patients were discharged and see if we can track down others who left on the same day. If there's an infected pack of dressings in the hospital. . .'

Looking down at Kala's worried face, she left the sentence unfinished, unwilling to raise any more spectres in her friend's mind.

'I'd better fly. It seems there's more than one disaster hovering over our heads tonight!'

She grinned reassuringly at Kala, but the problem of the dressings—definitely a nursing concern—and Gabe's cool summons worried her more than she would willingly admit.

'Glad you could make it,' Mark said with mocking sarcasm when she finally entered the theatre, gowned and gloved, but with her mind still engaged with Kala's puzzle.

She glanced briefly from him to Gabe, who was watching her with eyes that looked like blue glass, so clear and expressionless that she wondered if she could have imagined their twinkling, teasing, loving beauty.

Right back to being professionals, she thought, hiding a small hurt part of herself under a similar façade. Then she noticed the figure in the shadows. So Arab money is still with us, she thought bitterly. Is that why I'm being treated like this? Is he afraid to show consideration to me in front of a man from a land where men do not openly acknowledge the contributions of their women?

'Who's the patient?' she asked, striving to regain her own professionalism.

'Anani!'

The one bleak word drove through to her heart, and she looked down at the slight figure.

'What's happened? What's gone wrong?'

'I think it's a haematoma beneath the second graft. Something's happening in there, because the graft isn't taking as it should.'

'Will you have to remove it?'

'Let's hope not. I'm going to make a small incision, then apply pressure and see what comes out. If there's a clot we should be able to remove it, but if it's infected fluid that's not draining to the edges we'll have to remove the sheet. . .'

'And she'll have to go through it all again.'

'It's a set-back, Leith, not the end of the world.'

Gabe spoke sharply, and Mark gave her a quick wink of sympathy, his eyes twinkling encouragingly at her over his mask.

It was a simple procedure that could have been done in Anani's room, were it not for the risk that infection was present, and a long and messy cleaning-up operation would be involved.

'It's blood,' said Gabe, his pent-up breath releasing

in a soft sigh. 'I'll pump more antibiotics in just in case, but I'm sure that's all it is.'

'Will you close that incision with a stitch?' Mark was showing appropriate interest.

'I think a tiny plastic strip will hold it together. That way we can still leave the wound open and keep an eye on the graft.'

The job was done, Gabe continuing to pass on his knowledge to his pupil. Was he also talking to impress the silent observer?

As she wheeled Anani into the recovery-room, Leith watched him take Mark by the arm, then turn to usher his guest out through the door. She heard his words as they left the theatre.

'Normally we can pick up these problems, because we see them through the translucent skin of the graft, but I'm finding, with dark-skinned people. . .'

As his voice trailed away she felt a spurt of annoyance. She'd known he was professional, but this professional?

Then her mind returned to her own problem — or Kala's, she supposed it was. But it was of grave concern. Should she have mentioned it to Gabe?

She finished her work swiftly, then went through to the small room Kala used as an office, to see her dark head bent over the record books.

'They were discharged different days!' Kala's voice was bleak, and her face grey with fatigue.

'You go to bed. I slept all the way back on the plane; I'll look through the records and see if I can find anything that matches.'

'Would you, Leith?'

'Only if you promise me you'll go straight to bed. I'll check on all of them before I turn in — so don't worry.'

As the door closed behind Kala Leith looked down at the desk, her eyes flicking from the record cards of the patients to the big day book they kept. There were six readmittances—and who knew how many other infected patients who hadn't reported back?

All she could do was check—go over every case until she found some clue or similarity which could tie them together and give them the lead they needed.

It was two hours before she closed the books with a worried sigh. Piles of card littered the desk, as she had pulled out the surgical case notes as well, to check on her burgeoning theory. There was a soft tap on the door. Was Gabe still at the hospital? Was he calling in to say goodnight?

Mark's head appeared.

'What are you doing here at this time of the night?' she asked incredulously. The Mark she had known, although conscientious enough, never put himself out too much for his patients.

'I've moved in.'

She gaped at him in astonishment.

'Plenty of spare rooms, or at least there were until we got this rush of infections.'

He sounded quite unconcerned about what she saw as a major problem.

'So, rather than live it up at the hotel with the eminent Dr Vincent, I decided to stay here with the poor people.'

He grinned seductively at her before adding, 'What's more, I'm closer to you, my love. I know you won't be able to resist my charms if I'm near you night and day!'

'You're sick!' she said shortly. 'You can't seem to understand plain English. It's over, Mark, and it's been over for a long time.'

'I don't believe you, Leith.' He looked down at her, his eyes narrowed and his handsome face unreadable. 'I might believe you if you were involved with someone else. In fact I think the boss rather fancies you. But your holding yourself away from any entanglement means only one thing to me——'

'Of all the egotistical, self-satisfied, smug individuals in this world,' she spluttered, 'you must really take the cake! If you believe that, you'll believe anything! Now take your inflated ego and get out of here; I'm busy!'

'I'm going, but remember——' he leered wickedly at her, his good humour completely unaffected by her words '—I'm just down the passage when you need me.'

Leith tidied up with a weary resignation. She would speak to Kala in the morning about her theories, and just hope that the culture turned up an identifiable infection that they could treat.

Mark's presence in the building was an added complication—one that she did not relish.

He was good-natured enough, but, like many people who had an abundance of charm and good looks, he was spoilt and inclined to react badly if his precious self-conceit was affected in any way. A quick shiver of apprehension shook Leith as she pictured his reaction to the news that she and Gabe were lovers!

She sighed tiredly, and headed for her room, Abu Dhabi and the magic of their time together as far away as the moon that threw a ghostly light over the quiet building.

'Come on, sweetheart, it's time good nurses were up and about, no matter how late they got to bed.'

Consciousness returned with a heavy languor. Leith forced open her eyes and stared blearily about her.

Her eyelids felt heavy and her lashes sticky, while an itching warmth on her arms and shoulders told her she must have caught more of the sun than she'd intended.

'What are you doing here?' she asked sharply when she regained some order in her senses.

Mark was seated on the edge of her bed, perched against the curl of her body with an intimacy that she found infuriating.

'Waking Sleeping Beauty with a kiss, of course,' he said brightly, bending his head to kiss her sleep-numbed lips.

'Renewing an old friendship?'

Gabe's voice cut through the room like a sword through butter, and Leith felt a searing anguish.

She knew, without any doubt, that there would be no explanation acceptable to this man, whose moral code saw love and marriage as inseparable entities.

'Oh, it was a bit more than friendship,' Mark replied in even tones. 'Old lovers, aren't we, darling?'

Leith's eyes closed, her body icy-cold under the thin cotton sheet. She felt the bed move as Mark lifted his weight off it, and heard their voices cease suddenly as the door closed behind them.

'Are you there, Leith?'

Kala's voice came anxiously through her misery, and she flung herself abruptly out of bed, splashing water on her tear-stained face as she called, 'I'll be with you in a minute, Kala.'

'I've got coffee in my office,' was the reply. So Kala was anxious to know if she had found anything.

Personal problems had no place in her mind, she thought angrily as she dressed with frantic haste. Forget them both, she told herself—at least until this mess is sorted out.

'Ugh!' The wry grimace of distaste could not be hidden as she downed a mouthful of the abhorrent brew that they called coffee in this place.

'You should have tea,' Kala said with little sympathy. 'We have very good tea.'

'I can't wake myself up with tea,' Leith explained, holding her breath while she took another mouthful and swallowed hurriedly. 'This stuff might taste revolting, but it seems to have the same effect as real coffee.'

Even as she spoke, a trick of memory wafted the smell of fresh coffee past her nostrils, and she was transported back to yesterday's breakfast on the terrace—with Gabe. . .

'Did you find any connection?'

The question brought her back to the present, and she put her cup carefully down on Kala's desk.

'It's only a mad idea, Kala, but you and Prakash may be able to follow it through.'

Kala's huge eyes questioned her anxiously.

'You know the trouble we've had with the different religions.' She spoke hesitantly, unsure of her ground.

'Of course,' said the Indian nurse, accepting unquestioningly the fact that different religions in India meant problems within a hospital, where food, bathing habits and even medications could be offensive to one patient yet acceptable to another.

'Well,' Leith continued, unwilling to give offence to her friend, 'the only link that I can see is that they are all men, and they are all Hindus.'

'So it's something different we did to them, or for them. . .'

Kala sounded puzzled as her mind went back over the nursing procedures that followed each operation.

'Or something they did after they left here,' Leith prompted. 'Wasn't there some special day—some celebration. . .?'

A hazy memory of those first hectic weeks niggled at the back of Leith's mind.

'I'll check. It's a start, at least. Thank you, Leith. Now you'd better get into that theatre or we'll all be in trouble. Gabe has already reduced the night sister to tears, and even Prakash is looking worried. Maybe your trip away did not go well?'

It was as close to probing as Kala would ever come, their lives outside their work still a mystery to each other.

'It was a successful op, but a bit tiring.'

Leith felt heat spreading through her as she uttered the words, and left the room with a hasty farewell.

'I'd like to see you when you finish in here. I'll be in my office.' Gabe dropped his mask into the rubbish receptacle, and nodded to Leith as he moved to the door.

An involuntary surge of pleasure shot through her, then she remembered this morning's scene and her heart sank.

Slowly she went about her tasks, automatically washing the instruments and stacking them on to their trays for the steriliser, then scrubbing down the trolleys and packing away the dressings.

For a few moments her mind left Gabe, to switch to Kala's problems. She shrugged off that worry. Kala and Prakash were handling the next stage of that, although, once the source was traced... Her mind drifted back...

Thanks to the presence of the shadowy Arab, she and Gabe had parted with no plans or pledges for the future. She had assumed that when the time arose they would resume the affair that had started so joyously in the Emirates. But after this morning...

As she brushed her hair and splashed water on her pink cheeks she wondered what he wanted, wondered how he had taken Mark's proclamation. Her feet dragged down the corridor; she was dreading the moment ahead.

'Here's some money for the job in Abu Dhabi!'

He pushed a slim envelope across the desk towards her, as if anxious to avoid physical contact.

'Is that all you wanted, Gabe?' she pleaded, her breath catching in her throat. Look up at me, she wanted to say, but then he raised his eyes, and looked into hers for a long moment, and she wished she hadn't seen the cold bleakness of that stony blue stare.

'I thought the money was of the greatest importance to you. Isn't that the reason you accepted my invitation?' Ice dripped from his voice, and Leith shivered in the small, hot room.

'You know that's not the only reason I went,' she said in a small, stifled voice that she could barely hear herself.

'Oh, I know that now. I think Dr Armstrong made it abundantly clear.

'But Gabe——' she begged, but that arctic voice continued.

'You made no commitment to me, Leith. At least you were honest enough to deny any love. I assume our little fling has had the desired effect.'

'What do you mean, Gabe? What are you asking me?' she pleaded desperately, trying to find some sanity in his cutting words.

'It's brought our Dr Armstrong back into line, hasn't it? Once I realised the connection I remembered hearing some story about his breaking off with someone to take up with the lovely Caroline...'

She heard no more! She leaned forward and picked up the envelope with fingers that shook, but she refused to cry, or to beg or explain. He had said he loved her, but what was love without trust? Surely a very shallow emotion! She walked very quietly from the room, her eyes burning with unshed tears.

She couldn't sleep—might never sleep again, the way she felt! She had stayed on duty until midnight, sitting with Anani, then checking the feverish patients with the night sister, who was concerned by a lack of improvement. After three hours of futile tossing and turning, she climbed out of the rumpled bed and pulled a light cotton wrap over her flimsy night-gown.

'You might as well be doing something useful,' she told her reflection, as she brushed her hair, then turned out the light and left the room.

She went first to Kala's office, where she pulled out the cards she had studied the previous night and made a list of dates and numbers. Next she padded through to the dark, silent theatre, where she collected some small plastic bags.

The dressings were all kept in sterile packs in a room that might have been a pantry. Leith stared for a moment at their massed array, and said a silent prayer of thanks for the habit of nurses everywhere of opening new packs before they finished the old ones. With a sigh she consulted the notes she had made, and started work.

Taking one dressing from each of the open packs, she placed it carefully in a plastic bag. She sealed each bag, and numbered it to correspond with the pack, then shifted the open pack on to a top shelf.

She hoped that Kala had started using dressings from new packs as soon as the infection was discovered, but if she wanted to eliminate the hospital's dressings all the open packs would have to be checked.

Even if Prakash and Kala found some other answer to the problem, this was the only way they could convince the doubters that the hospital was not at fault.

She finished the job, her mind happy to be occupied with thoughts that didn't make tears flood her eyes! Some of the lower shelves were now bare, so she decided to clean out the small room while she was there, and for another hour she kept thoughts of Gabe at bay.

It was still dark as she made her way down the dimly lit corridor to her room, but a heightened sense of activity around her told her that the day had already begun. A shadowy male figure in white crossed the passage further down, and she realised that either Prakash or Mark must already be on duty.

She wondered briefly if they were always about this early, before turning into her room to gather up her uniform and head for a much needed shower.

CHAPTER NINE

LEITH remembered little of the next week. Two more men were admitted with infections, but the culture had isolated the bacteria and new antibiotics were now succeeding where the others had failed.

Anani's graft had taken, and the atmosphere in the theatre was no worse than working in Siberia with a group of deaf mutes, Leith told herself with a rueful sorrow.

'Gabe wants all senior staff in the old chapel when we finish.' Prakash attracted her wandering attention with a light touch on the arm. 'Could you delegate some of your tasks and come soon?'

He sounded agitated, and Leith saw his brown eyes scanning her face anxiously.

'Am I gaining a reputation for being late?' she asked him lightly.

'No, Leith,' he said quietly, 'but you are working too hard. You have lost all your sparkle!'

She turned away to hide a sudden spurt of tears. She could and would manage to get through the next two weeks in India—as long as no one's nice to me, she thought.

'I'll be right there,' she said swiftly, rushing into the changing-room to strip off her theatre clothes and rub some colour into her cheeks before following him to the lovely panelled room.

She slipped into a seat beside Kala, not looking

towards Gabe, who sat in a chair facing the rest of their small group.

I can avoid his eyes, but not his voice, she told herself as he started to speak, and the words were meaningless as she followed the deep cadence.

'It's fortunate that it didn't spread into grafts, and, although it seems to be contained, I feel we should go through all our procedures to make sure it doesn't recur.'

Leith shook her head, a puzzled frown twisting at her eyebrows. She was too tired to remember the details, but she was certain that Kala and Prakash had isolated the cause. She waited for one of them to speak, but they were both looking towards her, as if she should be the one to explain!

'Do you know something about it, Leith?' Mark asked the question. 'You looked into it when you got back from your trip.'

Some trip, she thought, but Gabe was looking at her impatiently, and the two Indians still sat mutely on their chairs.

'All I did was work out who had contracted the infection. Kala and Prakash followed up my idea.'

Were they worried about some religious aspect of this? she wondered. Was that why they refused to speak?

'You're not going to give me that rubbish about an infection that only strikes Hindus, are you? I've already told Prakash the idea's ridiculous. You can't blame a purely localised infection on different eating and praying habits.'

Hearing the smouldering fury in his voice, she realised why Kala and Prakash were holding their tongues.

'We're not completely stupid, Dr Vincent,' she said quietly, injecting an unconcerned coolness into her voice. 'But the fact that all those infected were male Hindus did seem to point to some connection.'

'Absolving the hospital of any blame? Is that what you're saying, Sister? Because dressings are a nursing problem, you're hurriedly trying to point us in some other direction.'

His bitter words hit her like small stones, and she found herself flinching back in her chair, but she was not going to be overawed by his unreasonable anger, and straightened up as she spoke again.

'We were very aware that it was a nursing problem. That's why we've eliminated the dressings as the source of infection.' She glared at him as she spoke, but her eyes dropped from his furious gaze to his hands—to those slender fingers worrying away at a pen as if they would never rest again.

'I knew I'd have to do that to convince the patients. It didn't occur to me that the medical staff would need similar assurances,' she added caustically.

'How did you eliminate the dressings?' he asked sharply.

The air in the room had thickened, she was sure of it! She struggled to breathe, battling the intimidation in his voice and the awful silence from the others. If the words of love he had once spoken were true, could he treat her like this? Could a simple misunderstanding lead to this much vindictiveness?

She'd survived another trauma through concentrating on her work, and she'd survive this one. She'd show Dr Gabe Vincent—show him how little he affected her!

As long as he doesn't take my pulse, she thought with a little imp of humour fighting through her gloom.

Suddenly aware of the silence in the room, she took a deep breath and went on to explain, 'I took one dressing from each opened pack, and Prakash sent them to the lab for testing. We checked back through the store records that no packs had been completely finished, so we knew we had the lot. . .'

Her voice had started to quiver. She hated having to justify her actions, hated this feeling of accusation that still hovered in the air. She wanted to run —

'When did you do this?'

Gabe's voice was sharp — insistent — and she thought tiredly back.

'It must have been the night after we came back. I couldn't sleep. . .'

Her voice trailed away, and she battled the tears that threatened to overwhelm her.

'Leith. . .?'

It sounded like a strangled plea, but she hadn't the strength to analyse it. She bowed her head over her hands and felt a rush of gratitude when she heard Prakash take over.

'I am sorry you felt you had to hold this inquisition, Gabe.' Prakash was enunciating each word with a carefully controlled anger. 'Sister Robinson had already done so much, finding the connection between the cases, and taking it on herself to have the dressings tested. She is not part of our nursing staff, and could easily have ignored the whole situation, but no, she worked with us.'

Leith was amazed to hear the correct young Indian speaking to Gabe this way, and she wondered how he was taking it. She cast a quick glance towards him from under her lashes, but his head was bowed over his hands which still twiddled so restlessly.

'When Prakash told you that all those infected were Hindus we had not checked any further.' This was mutiny indeed, thought Leith, as Kala took up the story.

'You should not discount what you do not know, Gabe,' she went on primly. 'Even with our own religion, it was Leith who gave the clue.'

'There *was* a festival?' Leith asked, suddenly remembering her vague feelings about the timing.

'Of course,' said Prakash with a touch of humour. 'When is there not?'

'You'd better explain, Prakash,' Gabe said in a tired voice, drained of all anger or emotion.

'It was a time of ritual bathing, but these men, they knew they must protect their grafts, so only bathed their lower bodies.'

'I don't believe it! Are you telling me that these men left the hospital and within days were plunging their bodies into one of those filthy temple pools?'

It was Mark who voiced the disbelief, but the expression on Gabe's face was proof that he was equally staggered by the idea.

'It is our way,' said Prakash with a solemn dignity that finished any further speculation or discussion.

There was an uneasy silence in the room, broken only when Mark said with an assumed ease, 'Well, if that's all, Gabe, I've some post-op patients to see.'

There was a shuffling of feet as they all shifted in their chairs, looking expectantly at Gabe.

'Can we include a warning against ritual bathing in the talk we give them before discharge?' he asked grimly, and Kala nodded, a pleased smile easing the strain in her face.

'We are already doing that,' she said quietly, and, as Gabe waved a dismissing hand, they all moved quickly from the room.

'Leith. . .'

Did she hear him call her name, or was it an echo in her ears? She kept moving forward, not stopping at her room to change, but letting her feet take her swiftly from that place, leading her without conscious thought to the beach.

Two more weeks, she thought, mentally reviewing the cases that still required surgery. We'll be finished within Gabe's estimate of two months, after all.

Two more weeks! Would she survive it? Could she continue to work so closely with this man, hearing his voice, watching his hands as they exercised their special skills, banishing the memories until she had time to cry?

She felt the soft sand beneath her feet, and thought about sitting down, but the tension within her would not allow her to rest, so she walked on, her mind battling to overcome her heart, her common sense telling her that it was all for the best.

If you'd had a long affair with him it would be even harder to make the break, it said, and her heart could not argue.

Having decided that you couldn't marry him, why get more involved? it asked, and again her heart had no answer.

You've got over worse things than this, it told her, but this time her heart demurred. Not worse, she thought, not worse than this.

* * *

As it happened, the two weeks passed so swiftly that it was only later, when she thought back, that she realised how much Prakash and Kala had helped. Whether they had guessed at her unhappiness, or because she had helped them with the infection problem, she would never know, but the two combined to see that every spare minute was filled.

She would come off duty to find they had plans for her to dine at one or other of their homes, to accompany them to a movie house or to visit another shrine or temple, even, one memorable evening, to see a performance of the Bharata Natyam, where the brilliant women dancers expressed their love for Krishna — symbol of the ideal man. The poignancy and eroticism of the dancing brought tears to Leith's eyes, and the empty agony of her desire became unbearable.

She saw little of Gabe outside the theatre. He was away from the hospital frequently, and when he was there seemed to be closeted in his office with a telephone or visitors. Mark was also busy, as the number of post-op patients grew steadily. She moved through each day with a set resolve — to reach the end of it, and bring her release one day closer.

'Been avoiding me?'

She was sitting in the staff dining-room. Anani's departure from the hospital meant that she no longer had a sanctuary.

'Not really, Mark,' she answered.

'What's wrong, sweetheart?' he asked with such gentle concern that she felt an irrational impulse to burst into tears.

Unable to reply, she shook her head, staring down

HEALING LOVE 167

at a plate of lamb and rice that had suddenly become inedible.

'Whatever it is that's bothering you, it would be better to talk about it,' Mark went on quietly, 'and don't bother telling me that there's nothing wrong. I've known you for a long time, remember.'

A faint heat coloured her drawn cheeks, and Leith felt her fingers trembling as she toyed with her dinner.

'It's just the work and the heat. I'll be fine when I get away from here.'

'Don't give me that, darling. You were working like a slave when I first arrived, and blooming with some inner beauty that made me realise how mad I'd been to break off our engagement.'

'That's all in the past,' she responded listlessly.

'I know that, and, believe me, I regret it, but I'm not trying to win you back now.'

He reached across the table and patted her hand, grinning sheepishly at her.

'I also know I'm a smug, egotistical and...what were the other words you called me?'

'I'm sorry, Mark. I was upset.'

'I know that too. That's what I'm trying to say to you, silly! If even a selfish so-and-so like me can see you're upset over something, then it must be serious. You're like a ghost around the place — even worse than you were after the accident.'

'I didn't think you'd even have noticed how I looked back then!' she said with a faint smile, remembering that awful time without the pain that the memories usually evoked.

'I'm not completely without conscience, love!' he protested. 'Now honestly, would you have fallen in love with a fellow who was a complete phoney?'

'Of course not,' he said, answering his own question as he saw her faint smile. 'So, having proved I have a caring side to my nature, shall we get back to the problem in hand? What's wrong with you?'

'Nothing that you or anyone else can do anything about, Mark,' she said finally.

'Is it to do with Gabe Vincent? He's been pretty unbearable to work with since your little trip away. Did he make a pass at you?'

Unable to trust her voice as Mark's probing began to rub at her sore heart, Leith shook her head.

'You're in love with the guy!'

He said it with the awe of someone who had seen a vision, and again Leith felt a wry amusement. Mark had never been one for self-analysis, and other people's feelings were a complete mystery to him, so any kind of perceptiveness must come as a shock!

'And I mucked it up for you that morning after your trip. Was he coming down to your room for a quick kiss and a cuddle?' He paused for a moment, as if reliving the scene, then added, 'And there I was bleating about being old lovers! Oh, sweetheart, I'm sorry. Did I ruin things between you?'

He reached out and took her hands, squeezing them tightly in his and rubbing their coldness as he sought her pardon.

'It certainly didn't help,' she told him wearily, 'but the whole thing had no future. It was probably just as well that it ended there and then.'

'But that's nonsense, Leith. Why should it have no future? He's a good man, earns a nice living, clean habits, I'm sure.' He mocked her gently. 'I'm certain he's also the type of man who thinks love and marriage go together — unlike some we could mention.'

That self-deprecating grin slid into place as he tried to raise another smile, but Leith's eyes were clouded with pain, and her voice refused to work.

'What more could any girl want?' Mark persisted.

He sat in silence for a few moments, and Leith could feel his eyes on her as she prodded viciously at her meal, moving it around on her plate with a determined intensity.

'I'll talk to him! I'll explain that it was a joke, tell him I offered my body to you for a brief Indian adventure, but had been refused. I'll tell him——'

'No, Mark!' she said with a desperate urgency. 'Please don't talk to him. Please don't do that. It wouldn't have worked out, so it's better that it stopped before it went too far. I'll get over it.'

'Why wouldn't it have worked out?'

Silence stretched between them, taut as a wire.

'Why, Leith? Tell me why.'

'Because I can't have children,' she blurted out, tears starting to trickle slowly down her cheeks. 'Why else?'

She lifted her head to look at him with the bitter question in her eyes.

'But surely if he loved you. . .'

'You loved me, Mark,' she said wearily. 'Men might say they marry for love, but in reality it's because they feel the need to reproduce themselves, to provide the world with little images of themselves. It's their stake in the future, and you know it.'

He could not deny it.

'Not all men feel that way!' he protested, but the words lacked conviction.

'Don't they, Mark?' She longed for him to deny her assumption, to convince her that children weren't important, but when he spoke his voice was doubtful, and she knew that she was right, whatever he said.

'Well, you don't know, do you? Have you told Gabe that you can't have children?'

'No, and I'm not going to, and nor are you. I mean it, Mark. I don't want him to know.'

'But I'd like to help you,' he begged. 'Isn't there something I can do? I hate to see you so unhappy.'

'I'll get over it, Mark,' she answered tiredly. 'That's one thing I know for certain. It will take time, but in the end it'll be just another memory.'

Whether because the talk with Mark had helped, or from sheer exhaustion, Leith slept well for the first time in weeks. She woke to a feeling of heightened activity in the building—an impression of slight alarm or urgency.

'What's happening, Kala?' she asked as she met the girl on her way back from the shower.

'Gabe wants to leave later today, and we're just reorganising the schedule for Prakash and Mark to finish up.'

'Gabe's leaving?' Despair flooded through her, and she realised that having him so close had been a nightmare, but not having him around would be even worse!

'There's been an earthquake in Turkey—and a fire—and the Arabs are supplying a plane——'

'What are you talking about, Kala?' she cried, shaking the girl's arm as she tried to comprehend what she was saying.

'It seems he's been trying to get a plane set up like a mobile burns unit, and now, although it wasn't all

HEALING LOVE   171

finalised, this earthquake has given them a chance to test out the idea.'

'Them?' she echoed stupidly, her brain refusing to function normally.

'Gabe and some other surgeons from all over the world, and, of course, the Arab people he's been talking to——'

'And he's going today? To where an earthquake's just been?' She could feel the panic rising within her body, and the first flutters of fear as Kala's words sank in.

The other girl just nodded.

'He'll need a nurse,' Leith said desperately. 'You'd manage without me?'

'If you want to be with Gabe, then of course you must go,' Kala said with a quiet authority.

Leith reached out and gave her a quick hug, then went swiftly down the corridor to Gabe's office.

Did she imagine a quick gleam of hope as he looked up from writing to see who had entered the room? Probably, she told herself, as he turned a blankly enquiring gaze upon her.

'Kala tells me you're going.' Now that she was here the words would not come easily—and his answering nod was no help!

'You'll need a nurse, and I'd like to come.'

'No!' he said with an explosive force that shook her conviction—but only momentarily.

'It's an emergency, Gabe. To help as many people in as short a time as possible, you need someone who knows your routine. Unless you plan to delay your trip while you fly in someone from Australia, then I'm it.'

'I won't take you!' he said positively, his knuckles

white as his fingers betrayed their agitation, bending a pen that had done little to deserve its fate.

'Hardly a professional attitude, Dr Vincent,' she said with a studied calm that belied the seething turmoil within. 'Surely you're not going to let personal considerations interfere with your professional life.'

'I'm leaving in four hours,' he ground out, flinging the now broken pen into the bin below the desk and raising his eyes to look at her with a mixture of anger and despair.

For a long moment those blue eyes looked at her, mesmerising in their intensity. Then he sighed.

'I don't want you so close to danger, Leith,' he said quietly.

'I feel the same way about you, Gabe, so we might as well both suffer.' And without another word she turned and walked out of the room.

She said her farewells with a great sadness, and packed a small bag. If they did not return to India, Mark would take the rest of her clothes back home when he left.

He came out to see them off, with Prakash and Kala. Other staff and patients lined the veranda, and a soft sigh went up as the car pulled up in the drive.

'Take care,' Mark said quietly, giving her a brief hug and handing her into the car. Gabe was already seated, his eyes fixed on the road ahead, his profile cold and forbidding.

'I was wrong about you and Mark, wasn't I?' he asked bleakly.

'Yes, Gabe.' She answered him coolly.

'I came to see you...the night after we came

back. . .' His face remained immobile, and he forced the words out past lips that were thinned with strain.

'I couldn't sleep. . .had to see you, touch you. . . You weren't in your room. . .' he muttered.

She let the words fall where they lay. Should she defend herself? No, she thought dejectedly, why help him?

Then the tension grew too great for her to bear!

'I couldn't sleep either,' she said flatly. 'I was checking the dressings!'

He nodded at her words.

'I saw you come back down the passageway. I thought. . .'

She remembered the shadowy figure in white that she had taken for Mark or Prakash, and so much became clearer.

'I know what you thought, Gabe,' she said lightly, but her throat was tight with unshed tears.

How stupid we must look, she thought as she stared fixedly through the front windscreen of the car, the two of us sitting here like stuffed dummies, unable—even with friendship—to bridge the yawning chasm that has opened up between us.

'I love you, Leith Robinson. Will you marry me?'

He spoke with a quiet desperation. She knew he had turned, at last, to look at her. She could feel his eyes scouring her face as if his glance were a rough physical caress. But she could not meet that look, could not stand her ground under his scrutiny.

'No, Gabe,' she said with such immeasurable sadness that his hand moved to her shoulder and he pulled her close.

'Don't sound like that, little one. I didn't mean to

bring you pain.' He sighed deeply, his restless fingers moving on her arm.

'I spoke of love, then proved myself unworthy of the word. I didn't trust. . . I was so jealous I thought I'd go mad. I wanted to kill him, Leith, and that frightened me, because I've always prided myself on my control.'

His voice faded to a whisper, but she was content to lie relaxed against his chest, while his hand stroked her with a soothing intimacy.

'Maybe. . .?' he asked, a glimmer of hope in his voice when she did not reject his caress.

'No, Gabe,' she said again, with a dreary finality, her heart breaking with the weight of her denial.

'OK,' he whispered, his lips buried in her hair, and through the tiredness and the aching emotion a faint flicker of arousal stirred deep inside her, and she pushed herself hurriedly away from him and patted her hair into place.

'We'll be too busy to be worried about love, Dr Vincent,' she said with a feigned lightness. 'For a start, you can tell me about this plane!'

She could see the traffic thinning as they left the city, heading for the airport, and heard Gabe's shuddering sigh as he drew breath, then answered her, the composure in his voice echoing her own.

'It's something that a group of us — from all over the world — have been planning for some time. The Red Cross and United Nations are geared up for a tremendous effort in all rescue work and can fly mobile hospitals and operating-theatres to trouble-spots fairly quickly.'

'Using Army equipment like our hospital?'

'Yes!'

She waited until he was ready to speak again.

'But they've never had the speciality gear needed to treat burns immediately.'

'Or the staff with the right skills, I imagine,' she added drily.

'Probably not,' he agreed. 'Anyway, at a conference in the United States last year a group of us decided to dedicate one third of our income for one year——'

'Which is why you had to make as much money as you could this year!'

She felt absurdly pleased at hearing the reason for Gabe's mercenary streak.

'Spot-on, little one! We had enough to equip a hospital when someone suggested that, instead of a tent theatre, we go for a flying theatre!'

'Flying theatre?' she asked, her mind boggling at the thought.

'A plane that was set up all the time—or one with the basic needs in place that could be converted easily.'

'Hence Aziz's father and his family,' she said, nodding in confirmation as it all fell into place.

'Well, they did have more than one plane,' Gabe said drily, and Leith chuckled.

'Just in case one wife wanted to shop in New York while another wanted to go to Harrods?'

'Something like that!' Gabe agreed. 'Anyway, after seeing our set-up here, Aziz's father agreed to put a plane at our disposal.'

'You're not going to be operating in that plush, carpeted motel on wings, surely?' she asked in disbelief.

'Well, I rather hope it's been altered somewhat. We'll know very shortly,' he added as the car turned into the airport and drove along a side-road to where the Arab family's plane stood waiting.

It was Nate who greeted them, taking their bags and giving Leith a quick hug.

'Good girl!' he said approvingly, 'I was hoping you'd be along on this trip.'

'Someone to do the cooking?' she joked.

'Nope,' he said seriously, 'that's mc. I'll be grounded while you two are using my bus as an operating-theatre, so I'll show you just how well we men can prepare meals.'

'How'd you get on with the refit?' Gabe asked as they climbed the steps into the body of the plane.

'See for yourself,' was the proud response as Nate waved an arm around the space where that ornate room had once been.

Gone were the carpets, gold paint and deep armchairs, and in their place was a pristine new theatre, slightly odd in appearance as the equipment was all fixed to the walls and the central space was empty.

'It all unstraps and rolls into place as soon as we touch down. That was the boss's idea—to fix it all to the walls rather than pack it in the hold. To save time, he said.'

He ran a hand proudly over the shining new fittings, then went on, 'And we've kept six seats up front for whoever is travelling with the plane—that's where you'll be this trip.'

'It's fantastic,' said Gabe, awe in his voice at what had been achieved in such a short time. 'But it means he's virtually given this plane over to us.'

'Not quite,' Nate answered, grinning at them both. 'In between natural disasters, we simply press this button...'

He did so, and long lockers on each side of the plane opened, and red velvet curtains rolled out along a track, completely concealing the medical paraphernalia.

'We throw a carpet on the floor, and blot the chairs back into place, and we still have a vehicle—slightly smaller than before, but still big enough to fit the whole family.'

'It's unbelievable,' Leith murmured, awed by this demonstration of what money could achieve.

'And through here——' Nate waved his arms in the manner of a tour guide '—we have destroyed one of the best bedrooms in the sky to make a little home away from home for the workers.'

It reminded Leith of a compact caravan. Four bunks lined the walls, and a door led off to what was obviously a bathroom. Next to that was a tiny galley kitchen.

'It'll be cosy,' said Gabe with a smile at the other two. 'But if we have time for sleep it'll be very welcome. You've done a great job, Nate, and I'm not the only one who'll be thankful.'

'Well, we're all cleared to go, so get up front to your seats and we'll be off. I've a young co-pilot with me, and we'll be stopping only once *en route*, so get whatever sleep you can; I've a feeling you'll be really busy once we hit that little city.'

He hid his pleasure at Gabe's praise with a spate of words, but his face had a rosy glow, and Leith could feel his pleasure.

They followed him forward and strapped into their seats under his watchful eye.

'Once we're up, you can go through to the bunks if you like. You'll find straps there to secure you if you want to sleep during the flight,' he told them.

'In my vast experience with international flights,' Leith said with a smile, 'I've never found a bed at all necessary for sleep. I can feel a yawn coming on just sitting here.'

'Well, spread out and be comfortable; it's a fair hop.'

He disappeared into the cockpit, and Leith was at once concious of Gabe's nearness, feeling the heat of his body warming against her side. Think about work, she chided herself.

'Do you know what to expect when we get there?'

'Only that when the quake hit it triggered a fire that swept through a very crowded part of the city. I imagine it was caused by a gas main being severed, but I really don't know any details.'

'And what will we do?'

'Well,' he said slowly, 'because most emergency aid comes in by air the headquarters is generally set up at the airport. It's generally assumed that the hospital will be affected, or will be flat out coping with its own problems, so a mobile hospital is always among the first things flown in, and it's usually set up close to the airport as well.'

'So we fly in and set up shop beside it.'

The idea filled her with wonder. Mind-boggling disasters occurred at regular intervals all over the world, but what staggered her was that this type of relief support could be mobilised so quickly.

'Spot-on, Sister Robinson! And because we're on the scene so early we can use grafts to close wounds immediately and cut down on all the risks of fluid loss and infection and the worst of the scarring.'

'What about the more superficial burns, Gabe? Surely not all those injured will be as badly affected as they were in the factory fire.'

'I hope not. We'll have to wait and see. The first- and certainly the less severe second-degree burns will be dealt with by the other medical staff, but the plane has burn suits, sleeves, masks and leggings, so we can help by fitting those when the wounds are healing.'

'Would a mask have saved Anani's face?' Leith could not forget the marred beauty of the young girl.

'It would have stopped all the puckering,' Gabe explained carefully. 'The pressure of the masks and suits reduces all of that, but the burns were so deep that she would probably still have needed grafts.'

He looked across at her, and for a moment she met his questing eyes. Then she turned to look out of the window, but Madras was gone.

'Why was Anani so special to you, Leith? What bond did you share with her to make you care so much?' He asked the questions with a tenderness that smote her heart, but she could not answer.

CHAPTER TEN

GABE's and Leith's patients came in a steady stream, borne by workers whose faces were ravished by the grief and suffering they had witnessed in their desperate bid to find survivors in the chaos of the city. At first Leith was physically ill, shocked by the stench and the hardness of the burnt skin and tissue, but she learnt to mask her feelings, handling the patients as carefully as she could as she soaked away their clothes and cleaned the areas of deepest injury ready for Gabe's attention.

Using local doctors and nurses as assistants in their tiny theatre, they fought for the lives of these strangers. All those with full-thickness burns were put on intravenous fluids as soon as they were brought into hospital, and their wounds were washed and dressed. Gabe had listed patients in order of importance, and took those with injuries to their hands and feet as a priority. By removing the necrotic tissue within forty-eight hours, he could use autografts of the patients' unburned skin to cover the area, preventing infection and further fluid loss.

'It's their hands and feet that are most likely to suffer from contraction if the wounds are left to heal themselves,' he explained to Nate as they sat over dinner one night.

'What about those with burnt faces, and the scarring they'll suffer?' Nate asked.

'They're next on the list, but if necessary we can do some more grafting later for those people.'

Nate looked perturbed, the extent of the disaster only too evident whenever he stepped out of the plane.

'It's such a messy business, excising the wounds to get rid of all the burnt tissue,' Leith explained to him as he shuddered at the horror of it all, 'and it causes massive blood loss, so as well as the drip for fluids they need blood, and that's in short supply.'

Gabe patched the patients up and passed them on, rarely leaving the plane, as other hands took over the post-op care.

Leith found their months in India had sharpened her skills. She followed his actions and anticipated his needs so well that their hands performed in harmony like the choreographed movements of dancers.

The tenor of their work had changed, as these patients' requirements were not for cosmetic surgery but often for life-saving emergency care. Leith watched in awe as Gabe cut into the wounds with speed and precision, preparing the burnt sites to receive their grafts. Her fingers obeyed his commands with alacrity as their working partnership denied the constraints of their personal lives.

Day turned into night and back into day, but the bright lights, fuelled by throbbing generators outside the plane, hid the changes, and only the cold heaviness of their bodies signalled the exhaustion that was seeping into their bones.

'We'll finish this graft, then snatch some rest,' Gabe finally decreed, admitting to a tiredness he had denied for too long. 'A few hours won't make a great deal of difference, and by the time we finish our next stint some relief should be on the way!'

Nodding to the local doctor to dress the wound, he

moved back from the table, and removed his mask. His face was grey with fatigue, and his pale lips white in his gaunt face. His thick black hair, squashed from the succession of caps, lay flat and lifeless against his skull.

Leith's heart went out to him as she longed to hold him in her arms and cradle that weary head against her breast.

'I'll be OK, little one,' he said, seeing the distress in her eyes. 'You let someone else scrub down and get some sleep yourself. You'll be quite safe from any unwanted advances,' he added, with a flicker of a smile.

But he's not amused, she told herself sadly — and nor am I. It was an uneasy truce in a battle of emotions that seethed and bubbled not far beneath the surface in each of them.

They slept, then ate, then worked, then slept again. The routine became established, broken only by Leith, who spent her spare moments in the makeshift hospital set up outside their plane.

The long hours and tiredness exacerbated the tension between them, which stretched to snapping-point several times.

'There's no need for you to do extra work out there,' Gabe told her crossly as the strain of the hours they were working started to affect both their tempers.

'I'm not working,' she answered crossly.

'It doesn't matter what you're doing,' was the curt response. 'You should be sleeping.'

'You can't control my life, Gabe Vincent,' she muttered, pushing past him to get out of the plane.

'Oh, I know that only too well, Leith,' he said bitterly, turning from her to lie down on his bunk.

In the hospital she nursed the children, holding them in her arms and cuddling them with a tender concern. Slowly she saw the dazed, glazed look of shock fade from their eyes, and felt their shattered confidence begin to build again.

She knew the resilience with which these little ones would bounce back, and was simply helping them along the path that they were taking. Did Turkey have some arrangements whereby outsiders could adopt their children?

She could not remember reading about it, although she had studied most of the literature on overseas adoptions. There was certainly a whole new batch of orphans looking for families after this disaster. Her dream held true, the one set point in the swirling tumult of emotions.

Other surgeons arrived and the schedule became less hectic until, ten days after their arrival, it was clear that their job was done.

'We'll leave the plane here, because an extra theatre will be very useful for the next few weeks,' Gabe explained to her as they sat over coffee in their tiny cabin.

'Do we walk home?' she asked mockingly, her words hiding a cold despair that was creeping through her veins where warm blood should flow.

'You probably could,' he answered seriously. 'You have depths of strength and courage that amaze me, Leith Robinson.'

'Don't be nice to me, Gabe,' she pleaded. 'Whatever strength I may have had is lacking at the moment, and if you're nice to me I'll probably cry.'

'We'll fly home,' he told her gruffly, his eyes fixed with concern on her pale face. 'The Red Cross are arranging our tickets. . .'

Had he finished what he was going to say? She bent her head, and rested it against her hand as she sat and waited.

'They're trying to get us out of here tomorrow to meet up with a flight from Athens the next morning.'

'Tomorrow?' she cried, knowing that a part of her life was about to end, a part of her soul about to die.

'Tomorrow,' he echoed softly, but his voice held a hope that she could not let him hold.

'If the flight goes through Perth I'll get off there,' she told him. 'It's time I went home.'

There was no joyful excitement, no tremor of anticipation in her words.

'Leith. . .?' The word was a plea, a desperate entreaty, but she shut her heart and mind against it and rose quietly to walk out through the rear door and over to the hospital.

Walking down the rows of beds, she paused to speak words of encouragement, but lingered longest with the children. She sat on their beds, avoiding the drip lines, splints and protective boxes that held them prisoner, and played finger games with them. She held them in her arms, cuddling and caressing them as she murmured words they could not understand.

At the very end, a battered cot pulled out of the rubble of the township held a small girl in a pressure suit, her face unmarked by the fire that had scorched her body.

Thick brown curls, singed by the flames, clustered about her face, and huge eyes, nearly black in their soft darkness, looked out from her dusky face with a gleam of welcome. Leith gathered the tiny body in her arms and pressed her face into the springing hair, while slow tears dampened its softness and an aching, craving need ravaged her body.

'I can't let you go, just like that!'

She had not noticed Gabe come in, hadn't sensed his approach, but he was there, his arms around her, holding her and the child in a protective embrace that shut out all the horrors and heartbreak that the world could throw at her.

He saw the tears that streamed down her face and he clasped her even tighter, whispering against her hair.

'What is it, my darling? What is it that's tearing you apart like this?'

She could not answer, could not say the words that would reveal her anguish.

'It's children, isn't it, Leith?' he asked, but with a new certainty in his voice. 'It's all to do with children, this refusal of yours to accept my love.'

She shook her head against his shoulder, denying him an answer, and all the while the tears flowed faster, and she could do nothing to stem the tide.

With his arm strong around her shoulders, he led her outside, the child still cradled against her body. Brilliant stars lit the night sky and the air was hot and dry, with the lingering smell of fire and dust still reminding the senses of man's insignificance in nature's plans.

'I found this seat a few nights ago, when I followed you out to the ward and saw you with the children.'

He pulled her down on to a rough concrete slab that lay forgotten on the ground.

'It's a good place to sit and think, or sit and talk, or just sit,' he told her with infinite tenderness.

Slowly the tears dried up and Leith felt the soothing calm of the evening wrap around her, as if tying her to Gabe with invisible threads.

'Tell me, Leith,' he demanded, with a quiet authority.

She sighed deeply, a breath of sound in the still night.

He would wait forever for her to talk, she thought, and as the child stirred in her arms, settling her head against Leith's breast to sleep, she found herself reliving the horrors of that day, and the torture of the days that had followed it, and she whimpered slightly, the sound coming from deep within her, as her body twisted in an anguished denial of the phantom pain.

'I was pregnant,' she said finally, her breath coming in shuddering gasps as she forced herself to utter the words that had shamed her so much.

Gabe sat in silence, not moving, his breath soft in her hair.

'I had an accident.'

She felt his arms tighten about her, and his body rock her soothingly.

'The baby was killed!' she cried, and then, in a final healing release of the festering, frightening truth, she added, 'I killed my baby, Gabe, killed it and then was punished.'

Frantic sobs racked her body as the full horror of her thoughts lay revealed between them, but Gabe's hold on her did not loosen and his gentle swaying movement continued to comfort her.

'Did you deliberately go out to have an accident? Was it a wild attempt at abortion or suicide?' he asked with a studied calm.

She raised her head to look at him, tear-drenched

eyes of pansy-brown large with horror as they searched his face.

'No, of course not.' She could not hide the shock in her denial, and hastened to explain, 'I wanted that baby so much, Gabe.'

Her throat hurt as she held back more tears. 'I longed to see it, to hold it in my arms and feel its tiny lips at my breast. It was like a magical gift.'

She felt his arms tighten as she whispered her declaration of love, and felt his lips against her hair.

'Then you didn't kill the baby, little one. It was an accident, nothing more.' He spoke with such conviction that she put aside her pain to listen to what he had to say. 'You're an intelligent woman, Leith. You *must* have known that! Why have you tortured yourself this way for so long?'

The silence grew between them.

I'm back at this point again, she thought sadly. I know he loves me, but love shouldn't have to be tested, shouldn't have to prove itself, shouldn't have to choose!

'Tell me, little one!'

He was so persuasive, so lovingly insistent!

She took a deep breath and blurted out the truth she feared so much.

'I can't have any more children.'

The painful words came out so suddenly that she heard them before she was conscious of having uttered them.

The cradling arms tensed, then relaxed as he shook her slightly.

'Oh, my little love, is that the reason you've tortured us both? The reason you won't say the words that I know are in your heart? Now you've told me that, tell me the rest,' he insisted. 'Tell me that you love me!'

'I love you, Gabe,' she answered, with a fathomless depth of feeling in her shaking voice, 'but I won't marry you and deny you the children that you should have.'

'Is that what this has been all about?' he asked with tender compassion in his voice. 'My foolish love! My heart! Do you really think that, with all the unwanted children already in this world of ours, I couldn't live without some biological replicas of myself?'

His arms released her and his hands slid across her back to grasp her shoulders and push her body away from him, so he could look down into her tear-stained face, glowing with an inner radiance in the soft light of the moon.

'I love *you*, Leith Robinson, not some mythical offspring you might have been able to produce. I love the gentle, loving, generous, sexy, beautiful, wonderful woman that is you, little one, and I want you as my wife, not as a mother for some hypothetical children.'

He bent his head and kissed her with infinite tenderness on her thirsting lips, his mouth sweet with passion. She felt her breathing quicken and her pulses race, spreading the liquid fire his touch could ignite coursing through her veins.

'Will you marry me, Leith Robinson?'

The question brought her back to earth with a thud. There was another hurdle to jump—another decision to force on Gabe.

'I still want children, Gabe,' she told him. 'I know that life would not be complete for me without them. I want to be a mother.'

'And you shall be, my little love. My wife, first, last

and always.' His kiss was a pledge of a love that would last forever. His lips moved across her face, to linger on her swollen eyelids, and smooth away the furrows on her brow. 'With that rare talent that most women seem to possess, my heart, I am certain you can combine two jobs, and be my wife as well as the mother of our children.'

He paused again, a pause that was filled with love. She sat at peace in his arms until she heard his voice again, hoarse with a rough emotion, as he breathed his final words of love. 'The children of our hearts.'

NEW from...

MILLS & BOON

HEARTS OF FIRE
by Miranda Lee

Welcome to a new and totally compelling family saga set in the glamorous world of opal dealing in Australia.

Laden with dark secrets, forbidden desires and scandalous discoveries. HEARTS OF FIRE unfolds over a series of 6 books as beautiful, innocent Gemma Smith goes in search of a new life, and fate introduces her to Nathan Whitmore, the ruthless, talented and utterly controlled playwright, and acting head of Whitmore Opals.

BUY ONE GET ONE FREE!
As a special introductory offer you can buy
Book 1 - 'Seduction & Sacrifice'
along with
Book 2 - 'Desire & Deception'
for just £2.50

Available from April 1994
Price: £2.50

Available from W. H. Smith, John Menzies, Volume One, Forbuoys, Martins, Woolworths, Tesco, Asda, Safeway and other paperback stockists.
Also available from Mills & Boon Reader Service, FREEPOST, PO Box 236, Croydon, Surrey CR9 9EL. (UK Postage & Packing free)

ON CALL!
Win a year's supply of 'Love on Call' romances ABSOLUTELY FREE?

Yes, you can win one whole year's supply of 'Love on Call' romances! It's easy! All you have to do is convert the four sets of numbers below into television soaps by using the letters in the telephone dial. Fill in your answers plus your name and address details overleaf, cut out and send to us by 30th Sept. 1994.

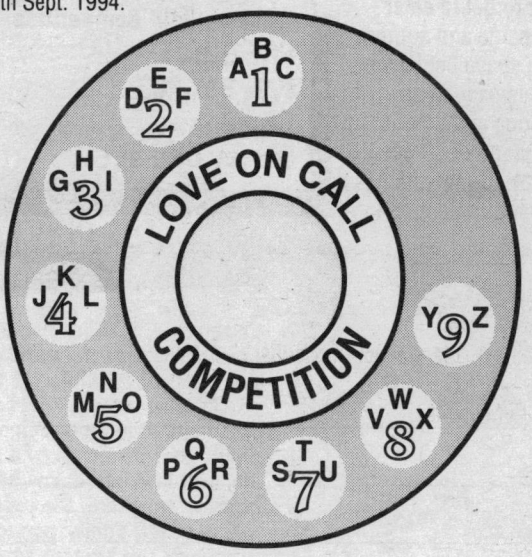

1 5233315767 _____

2 3552 152 1819 _____

3 165547322 _____

4 2177252267 _____

Please turn over for entry details

MILLS & BOON READER SERVICE COMPETITION!

ON CALL!
SEND YOUR ENTRY NOW!

The first five correct entries picked out of the bag after the closing date will each win one year's supply of 'Love on Call' romances (four books every month - worth over £85). What could be easier?

Don't forget to enter your name and address in the space below then put this page in an envelope and post it today (you don't need a stamp). Competition closes 30th Sept. '94.

'Love on Call' Competition
FREEPOST
P.O. Box 236
Croydon
Surrey CR9 9EL

EPLQ

Are you a Reader Service subscriber?   Yes ☐   No ☐

Ms/Mrs/Miss/Mr

Address

Postcode

Signature

One application per household. You may be mailed with offers from other reputable companies as a result of this application. Please tick box if you would prefer not to receive such offers. Offer valid only in U.K. and Eire.